Dearest Sabrina, she read.

This is hard for me to write, and I know it will be painful for you to read. There's no easy way to say it, so I'll just say it outright.

Six years ago I fell in love with a woman I met while conducting a tour in Italy. I couldn't seem to help myself. I know she would never keep seeing me if she knew I was married, so I pretended I wasn't. I told her I was divorced.

After we'd been seeing each other for a while, she began to press me for a commitment. I tried, but I couldn't give her up. So we got married.

I am so sorry for the hurt I've caused you,
Love,
Dad

Married!

Daddy, how could you have done this to us?

Dear Reader,

As you take a break from raking those autumn leaves, you'll want to check out our latest Silhouette Special Edition novels! This month, we're thrilled to feature Stella Bagwell's *Should Have Been Her Child* (#1570), the first book in her new miniseries, MEN OF THE WEST. Stella writes that this series is full of "rough, tough cowboys, the strong bond of sibling love and the wide-open skies of the west. Mix those elements with a dash of intrigue, mayhem and a whole lot of romance and you get the Ketchum family!" And we can't wait to read their stories!

Next, Christine Rimmer brings us *The Marriage Medallion* (#1567), the third book in her VIKING BRIDES series, which is all about matrimonial destiny and solving secrets of the past. In Jodi O'Donnell's *The Rancher's Daughter* (#1568), part of popular series MONTANA MAVERICKS: THE KINGSLEYS, two unlikely soul mates are trapped in a cave…and find a way to stay warm. *Practice Makes Pregnant* (#1569) by Lois Faye Dyer, the fourth book in the MANHATTAN MULTIPLES series, tells the story of a night of passion and a very unexpected development between a handsome attorney and a bashful assistant. Will their marriage of convenience turn to everlasting love?

Patricia Kay will hook readers into an intricate family dynamic and heart-thumping romance in *Secrets of a Small Town* (#1571). And Karen Sandler's *Counting on a Cowboy* (#1572) is an engaging tale about a good-hearted teacher who finds love with a rancher and his young daughter. You won't want to miss this touching story!

Stay warm in this crisp weather with six complex and satisfying romances. And be sure to return next month for more emotional storytelling from Silhouette Special Edition!

Happy reading!

Gail Chasan
Senior Editor

Please address questions and book requests to:
Silhouette Reader Service
U.S.: 3010 Walden Ave., P.O. Box 1325, Buffalo, NY 14269
Canadian: P.O. Box 609, Fort Erie, Ont. L2A 5X3

Secrets of a Small Town

PATRICIA KAY

Silhouette®

SPECIAL EDITION™

Published by Silhouette Books

America's Publisher of Contemporary Romance

This book is dedicated to all the wonderful people
in Struthers, Ohio, the small town where I grew up.
You're the best!

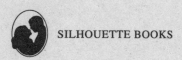 SILHOUETTE BOOKS

ISBN 0-373-24571-8

SECRETS OF A SMALL TOWN

Copyright © 2003 by Patricia A. Kay

This edition published by arrangement with Harlequin Books S.A.

® and TM are trademarks of Harlequin Books S.A., used under license.
Trademarks indicated with ® are registered in the United States Patent
and Trademark Office, the Canadian Trade Marks Office and in other
countries.

Visit Silhouette at www.eHarlequin.com

Printed in U.S.A.

Books by Patricia Kay

Silhouette Special Edition

*The Millionaire and
  the Mom* #1387
†*Just a Small-Town Girl* #1437
†*Annie and the Confirmed Bachelor* #1518
  Secrets of a Small Town #1571

Books previously published as Trisha Alexander

Silhouette Special Edition

Cinderella Girl #640
When Somebody Loves You #748
When Somebody Needs You #784
Mother of the Groom #801
When Somebody Wants You #822
Here Comes the Groom #845
Say You Love Me #875
What Will the Children Think? #906
Let's Make It Legal #924
The Real Elizabeth Hollister... #940
The Girl Next Door #965
This Child Is Mine #989
*A Bride for Luke #1024
*A Bride for John #1047
*A Baby for Rebecca #1070
Stop the Wedding! #1097
Substitute Bride #1115
With This Wedding Ring #1169
A Mother for Jeffrey #1211
†*Wedding Bells and Mistletoe* #1289

†Callahans & Kin
*Three Brides and a Baby

PATRICIA KAY,

formerly writing as Trisha Alexander, is the *USA TODAY*
bestselling author of more that thirty contemporary
romances. She has three grown children, three adored
grandchildren and lives in Houston, Texas, with her husband and their three cats. To learn more about her, visit
her Web site at www.patriciakay.com.

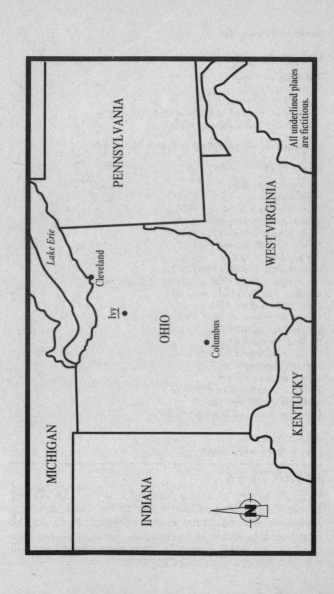

All underlined places are fictitious.

Chapter One

Sabrina March leaned back in her chair and sighed with satisfaction. "The chicken and dumplings were wonderful, as usual." She smiled at Florence Hillman, her parents' longtime housekeeper, who had begun to clear the table.

"Glad you enjoyed them." Florence's return smile was affectionate.

"I believe I enjoyed them far too much," Sabrina's father said, patting his stomach. "What do you say we go for a walk, Sabrina? Work off some of these calories." Turning to Sabrina's mother, he said, "You don't mind, do you, dear?"

Isabel March's gray eyes seemed, if anything, to grow frostier, but after a moment, she shook her head. "As long as you're not gone too long." Under her breath, she added, "I get little enough of your time."

As always, Ben March ignored her critical comment, and his voice was gentle as he replied, "I'll be back in an hour, no longer."

Sabrina's father, who was the CEO of his tour company, was due to leave on an extended trip—this time to Greece, Sabrina thought—early the following morning. His expertise lay in finding new areas to tour, then negotiating the best deals with hotels, restaurants and tourist attractions. March Tours wasn't a large company, but it was very successful in the high-end tour business. That success was directly attributable to her father's work ethic, which had translated into long absences from home.

These absences had been hard on Sabrina and her mother, so Sabrina sympathized with her mother's wish to have more of her father's attention. Even so, she couldn't help being glad she'd have a little time alone with him today. She loved her mother, but she adored her father.

When he was home, there was an excitement and cheer that was in short supply at other times. There was no one she respected more. In Sabrina's eyes, Ben seemed the ideal man: honest, hardworking, loyal, generous and loving. The past sixteen years couldn't have been easy ones for him, but he had never complained. In fact, his behavior had been an inspiration to her.

With only a nod to indicate she'd heard him, Sabrina's mother pushed back from the table. Her motorized wheelchair—the best money could buy— moved as silently as a cloud. If only her mother hadn't had that accident sixteen years ago, things might have been so different. *She* might have been different.

Sometimes Sabrina thought she couldn't stand her mother's unhappiness and bitterness another day. And then, as soon as the thought formed, she felt guilty for the selfishness of it. After all, it couldn't be easy for her mother who, before the skiing accident that had cost her the use of her legs, had been athletic and active. To compensate for these occasional uncharitable feelings, Sabrina tried to be doubly attentive and compassionate toward her mother.

"Ready?" her father said now, rising from the table.

Sabrina nodded, eager to be outside in the fresh October air.

Once they were in her father's car and on their way, he said, "Have you done any more thinking about your job since we last talked, honey?"

Sabrina sighed. "Yes, but I haven't come up with any answers."

He reached over and squeezed her hand. "Do you want me to talk to your mother about it?"

For just one weak moment, Sabrina was tempted. Then she sighed again. "No, Dad. This is my problem. I appreciate that you're willing to do it, but I have to handle this myself.''

Sabrina was the publisher of *The Rockwell Record,* the daily newspaper, which had been founded by her great-grandfather, Francis Kipling Rockwell. From the time she was old enough to understand what a newspaper was, she'd wanted to work there. But her vision had been romantic. She'd seen herself as a reporter or as the editor. She'd never wanted to run the business, to be the one who would hire and fire, the one who would have all the practical and financial worries. Yet since her Uncle Frank had retired, she was the only Rockwell left to head the paper. More and more, she'd had to leave the reporting and editing to others. For the past year, she'd been torn by a sense that her life had somehow gotten out of her control. And she felt powerless to change that.

''If I wasn't gone so much, and you didn't have the responsibility of your mother, too…'' her father began.

''It's not your fault. I don't want you to feel guilty. You know Mom would be very unhappy if you didn't bring in the kind of money you do. Besides, it wouldn't matter. She expects certain things of me, and that wouldn't change even if you were home all the time.'' She gave him a reassuring smile. ''I'm okay. Really I am. Now, let's talk about something else.''

Ten minutes later, car parked, Sabrina and her father began to climb the hill leading to the flower gardens of the park, which was their favorite place to walk. The path was strewn with brightly hued leaves from the maple trees that lined the walkway. Sabrina took a deep, appreciative breath. She loved autumn. It was her favorite season.

"Did you hear about what happened to Shorty Carwell last—" She stopped in mid-question. "Dad?"

Her father had abruptly stopped walking and was gripping his chest.

"Dad?" she said more urgently. "What's wrong?"

He grimaced. "Just…just a bit of…indigestion. Shouldn't have had that second helping of dumplings."

"Are you sure?" Sabrina didn't like his color. Normally her father's complexion was ruddy, but right now he looked pale. "Maybe we should go home."

He shook his head. "No, I'm fine. It's just indigestion. Walking will be good for me."

"But—"

"It's okay. I feel fine now." Smiling, he held out his arm.

Although Sabrina took it, she couldn't banish the kernel of anxiety that had knotted in her stomach. Maybe it was just her questioning nature—so valuable to a reporter—but his smile seemed strained to her. Yet he seemed determined to act as if nothing had happened, so she forced a lightness into her voice that she didn't feel.

"What time is your flight tomorrow?"

"Noon."

"So you'll be leaving early."

Her father always flew out of Cleveland rather than Akron, which was closer to Rockwell, because there were more flights to choose from. When Ben didn't immediately answer, she looked at him sharply. Alarm caused her heart to lurch. His face was now a ghostly white, and beads of perspiration stood out on his upper lip, although the late afternoon air was chilly. "Dad! You're *not* all right!"

"I—" He staggered back. Clutched his chest. His eyes met hers for one panicked moment. Then, with a strangled cry, he collapsed on to the walkway.

Sabrina lunged for him, but she couldn't hold on—he was too heavy. With a calmness she later marveled at, she whipped out her cell phone and punched in 911, as she sank to her knees and put two shaking fingers of her other hand against her father's carotid artery. She swallowed. There was no pulse. *Dear God.*

The moment she'd finished giving the emergency dispatcher the information that would bring an ambulance and EMT personnel to the park, she began CPR. Thank God she'd taken the lifesaving course only months earlier, as part of a series she'd done on emergency facilities in the area; otherwise, she wouldn't have had any idea how to go about trying to revive him.

"Dad, please be okay. Please be okay."

Over and over she pleaded with him even as exhaustion began to make it harder and harder to keep going. Again and again she went through the cycle she'd been taught. Fifteen compressions followed by two slow breaths into his mouth. Recheck his pulse. Fifteen more compressions, two slow breaths. Check the pulse.

By now she was sobbing with fright and frustration. No matter what she did, he still wasn't breathing! Where *was* that ambulance?

Please hurry, she prayed. *Please hurry.*

Finally she heard the wail of the siren, faint at first, then louder and louder as it pulled into the parking lot below.

Within moments, three EMTs converged on her. Strong hands moved her aside, and the technicians took over.

The next ten minutes were a blur. Sabrina watched numbly as the EMT personnel worked on her father. When one of them—a stocky dark-haired man who seemed to be in charge—called for the defibrillators, Sabrina bit her lip to keep from crying out.

Please, God. Please don't let him die. I need him.

She watched in agony, wincing each time they shocked her father's heart.

And then, in a slow-motion moment Sabrina knew

she would remember the rest of her life, the dark-haired EMT raised his head.

"It's no use," he said, looking at the other two.

"No!" Sabrina cried.

The female EMT turned to her. "I'm so sorry." Her dark eyes were filled with sympathy. "There's nothing else we can do. He's gone."

Sabrina stared at them. Her father *couldn't* be dead. He was only fifty-eight years old. He was way too young to die. "Daddy…" Tears ran down her face. "Daddy."

The female EMT stood, putting an arm around Sabrina's shoulder. She led Sabrina to a nearby bench. "Is there anyone I can call for you?" she asked kindly.

Sabrina numbly shook her head. Her father had no family. His parents were dead, and he had been an only child. And her mother…*dear God, her mother*…

"Are you sure?"

Sabrina wasn't sure about anything. "M-my mother's in a wheelchair. I—I have to go there and…and tell her." Oh, dear heaven. What was going to happen to them? How would her mother handle this?

"Is there any other family? Someone who can be with you so you don't have to do this alone?"

There was only her mother's brother Frank, but he was in poor health and retired with his wife in Florida, and her Aunt Irene, her mother's sister, who lived with her family in Savannah. Sabrina bit her trembling lip. *Casey. Casey would come.*

"I —I'll call a friend," she finally managed. Casey Hudson had been her best friend since high school, the closest friend she'd ever had.

The moment she heard Casey's voice, Sabrina broke down. Gently the EMT—whose name tag identified her as J. Kovalsky—took the cell phone out of her hand. In soft tones, she explained the situation. By the time Sabrina had regained control of herself, the phone call had been disconnected.

"Your friend said she'd be here in ten minutes."

Sabrina sat numbly as the two male EMTs loaded her father's inert body onto a rolling stretcher that they placed in the ambulance. "Wh-where will you take him?"

"To the morgue at County General."

Because of her newspaper work, Sabrina knew that a death certificate would have to be signed, and that her father's body would be kept at the morgue until whatever funeral home she and her mother chose would claim it.

Her lips trembled. Body. Morgue. Funeral home. They were such harsh words. Harsh and alien and final. Suddenly the numbness that had kept her grief in check evaporated.

Burying her face in her hands, she allowed the tears to come.

"Ashes to ashes, dust to dust..."
Sabrina listened to the words of the minister with

the same stoic acceptance she'd worn for the past three days. Everything that had happened since her father's fatal heart attack was a big, mixed-up blur in her mind.

Giving her mother the bad news. Making decisions about the viewing and the funeral. Notifying relatives and friends. Listening to all the expressions of sympathy on the phone and in person. Greeting everyone who came to the funeral home to pay their respects— hundreds and hundreds of people—a testament both to her family's prominence in Rockwell—her mother had been a Rockwell before her marriage to Sabrina's father—and to the fact that Ben March had been well liked by everyone.

And today, the funeral itself.

It seemed ironic to Sabrina that today should be such a beautiful one—crisp and cool, with a clear blue sky and golden sunshine gilding everything it touched. People weren't supposed to be buried on a day like this. Burials should take place on dark, gloomy, rainy days.

The minister dribbled a handful of dirt over the bronze coffin. "Benjamin Arthur March, we commit your earthly remains to…"

Sabrina tuned out the rest of the words. They were meaningless. Nothing anyone said would change a thing. Her father was dead.

She wished she were anywhere else but here. She didn't want to remember her father like this. Didn't want to see his coffin lowered into the ground. Didn't want to believe she would never see him again.

Her eyes burned with unshed tears. She hadn't allowed herself the luxury of crying since those few minutes in the park.

What good would crying do?

Her father was gone. Never again would she see his smile. Never again would he bring his optimism and good humor home. Never again would she feel the comfort and support of his strength.

Oh, Daddy, what will I do without you?

Next to her, her mother stirred. Sabrina glanced sideways. Isabel's profile was calm and dignified, her chin raised, her posture straight.

"Rockwells don't air their emotions in public," she'd said more times than Sabrina could count.

Resentment bubbled inside. Her mother hadn't broken down once. Not once. Not even when Sabrina had given her the news, a fact that had shocked Sabrina and made her wonder if her mother had *ever* loved her father. Then she felt guilty. She knew she shouldn't judge her mother simply because Isabel didn't show her grief the way Sabrina showed hers.

It wasn't just that her mother was a Rockwell and felt she had a certain position to live up to. Isabel had never been able to show her love easily. Some people were like that. They held their emotions inside, unable to share them. It didn't mean they didn't feel them.

Only once had Sabrina ever seen her mother lose

control. It was a memory long buried, but today it surfaced and Sabrina remembered how, as a twelve-year-old, she had heard her parents arguing.

She'd been upstairs in her room studying and the raised voices had drawn her to the top of the stairs. Ben and Isabel had been in the library—which was on the first floor near the stairway—and the door had been partially open. Neither had noticed, so caught up in the storm of emotion that their usual caution when Sabrina was nearby had been forgotten.

"It'll be a cold day in hell before I give you a divorce," her mother had been saying.

Sabrina had gasped, her hand flying to her mouth. Divorce! No! Not her parents. They *couldn't* get a divorce.

"Isabel, be reasonable," her father said. "Whatever love we once felt for each other is gone, and you know it."

"Rockwells do not divorce."

"Just to save face, you'd rather be miserable the rest of your life, is that it?"

"Who says I'll be miserable?" her mother had shot back. Then she'd stalked out, heading for the stairs, and Sabrina had scrambled to get back to her room before her mother discovered her listening.

That night Sabrina's father hadn't been home for dinner, and the next day her mother had left for a skiing trip. The skiing trip where she'd had the disastrous accident that had so affected the rest of her life.

From that day on, Sabrina's father had been a devoted husband. No one would ever have known the March marriage had been on the brink of dissolving, not from Ben's actions and certainly not from Isabel's. In fact, over the years, Sabrina had often wondered if she'd imagined that whole scene in the library.

Today, though, she knew she hadn't. No, her father's patience with, compassion for and devotion to her mother had been his penance. For Sabrina knew he'd blamed himself for the accident, even though he hadn't been there and hadn't caused the accident physically.

Nevertheless, she was sure he felt responsible, because if her mother hadn't been so upset, she wouldn't have been foolhardy enough to ignore the warnings and ski in conditions that were less than favorable.

Sabrina sighed. It wasn't right to judge her mother. Until you walked in another's shoes, you couldn't know how you would behave in similar circumstances.

Dad wouldn't want me to be bitter toward her, she thought. If he were here right now, he'd tell me he was depending on me to be understanding and kind, that Mom will need me now more than ever.

As that realization sank in, Sabrina could feel the weight of the future pressing down upon her. Now she could never leave the newspaper. Never try something different. Never have a life of her own.

* * *

After the last of the food had been eaten and all the guests had finally gone home, Leland Fox, her parents' longtime friend and the family's lawyer, asked if they were up to going over Ben's will.

"If you're too tired today, we can do it another day," he said gently, smiling down at Isabel.

"No, let's get it over with."

Sabrina would have preferred to wait, but the decision was her mother's, so she settled herself in a chair and waited for Leland to dig the will out of his briefcase.

"I'll just go give Florence a hand in the kitchen," Sabrina's Aunt Irene said. She smiled at Sabrina, then left the room.

There were no surprises in the will. The family home had belonged to Isabel's parents. After their death, she had bought out Frank's and Irene's shares, so the house was already in her name. Her and Ben's bank accounts and investments were held jointly with survivorship benefits. As for Ben's company, Sabrina and Isabel already held twenty-four percent of the stock apiece. Of the remaining fifty-two percent, eighteen percent belonged to Bob Culberson, Ben's general manager, and thirty-four percent was in Ben's name with the provision that upon his death, any stock held by him would be divided equally between Isabel and Sabrina.

In addition, there were two cash bequests: one to Florence and one to Jennifer Loring, Sabrina's cousin and the daughter of Irene.

For a few moments, Leland discussed the logistics of transferring money and stock, then he kissed Isabel goodbye and Sabrina walked him to the front door.

As he was putting on his coat, he dropped his voice and said, "Sabrina, could you stop by my office in the morning? I need to see you about a private matter."

"Of course." She wanted to question him, but she could see he didn't want her mother to know about this, so she only said, "What time?"

"Ten?"

"All right." Standing in the open doorway, she watched as he got into his car and drove off. What could he want that couldn't be said in front of her mother? A bequest, perhaps, that her father wanted kept secret? That seemed unlikely, but it was all she could think of.

For the rest of the day, as she helped Florence clean up after their guests, as she tended to her mother and helped get her ready for bed, and as she finally had some time to herself and was able to take a soothing bath before climbing into bed in her old room—she was staying at her mother's for a few days—she thought about Leland Fox's request and wondered what it involved.

The next morning, as soon as breakfast was over and her mother and aunt were ensconced in the sunroom with a pot of tea and their knitting, Sabrina said she had some errands to run and would be back for lunch. She kissed her mother's cool cheek with only a twinge of guilt.

She arrived at Leland's office, conveniently located next to the courthouse in the town square, ten minutes early.

"He'll be with you shortly," said Betty Treehorne, his longtime secretary.

Sabrina settled herself on to one of the burgundy leather sofas. Less than five minutes later she was ushered into his office.

"Have a seat, my dear," Leland said. He stood— a tall man with dark hair turning gray and friendly blue eyes—until she was seated in one of the chairs flanking his desk. Only then did he sit, too. "How are you holding up?"

Sabrina shrugged. "Okay."

"And your mother?"

"She's doing all right. Aunt Irene is going to stay for a couple of weeks."

"That's good. The next months are going to be hard for you both."

His kind face was almost Sabrina's undoing. But she fought the tears that hovered and managed to subvert them.

"Well…" He seemed at a loss. "You're probably wondering why I asked you to come to the office."

Sabrina waited.

He opened a file that lay on his desk and removed an envelope. "Your father left this letter in my safekeeping. He asked me to give it to you should anything happen to him.''

Sabrina's hands shook as she reached for the letter. Her heart felt as if it might burst. Her father had written her a farewell. It was so like him to know how much she would need to know he had been thinking about her and wanting to ease her grief.

She didn't open the letter in Leland's office. Instead, she headed for the park, thinking that would be a fitting place to read her father's final message to her. Even after arriving and settling on their favorite bench next to the rose garden, she didn't open the envelope.

She looked at the seal, looked at her father's handwriting—the bold letters and black ink. She traced the letters with her finger, then held the envelope close to her heart for a long moment.

Then, with a tremulous smile, she put her index finger under the sealed flap and slit it open.

Chapter Two

The letter was dated November, two years earlier.

Dearest Sabrina, she read.

Her father went on to say how much he loved her and how sorry he was to cause her pain, but there was something important she needed to know.

> *This is hard for me to write, and I know it will be painful for you to read. There's no easy way to say it, so I'll just say it. Six years ago I fell in love with a woman I met while conducting a tour in Italy.*
>
> *I couldn't seem to help myself. I knew she would never keep seeing me if she knew I was*

married, so I pretended I wasn't. I told her I had been, but I was divorced. I told her my name was Ben Arthur. She had no idea I owned the tour company. I told her I was a consultant who worked for a dozen different companies, both in the U.S. and abroad.

After we'd been seeing each other for almost a year and she began to press for a permanent commitment, I tried, but I couldn't give her up, so we were married in Las Vegas and honeymooned in Italy.

Sabrina gasped.

Married!

He couldn't mean that. Her father was *already* married to her mother. How could he marry someone else?

She and I have had two children together. Sabrina, I know how this must shock and hurt you, but please believe me when I say that what I feel for Glynnis and our children takes nothing away from what I feel for you. You are my first and will always be the beloved child of my heart. But I love little Michael and Olivia, too, and I know you will love them as much as I do after you get to know them. As I write this, Michael is three and a half, and Olivia is just a month old.

If you are reading this, I am dead, and there

will be no one else to take care of some things that must be taken care of. I could have asked Leland to do them for me, but it's going to be painful enough for Glynnis to discover not only that she's a widow but the truth about our marriage, so I was hoping you could find it in your heart to go and see her and tell her everything in person.

Sabrina read the letter three times before it really sank in. Her father was a bigamist. The man she'd admired and respected and thought so honest and upright and loyal and straight was a liar. He had betrayed her mother and her and everyone they knew.

How had he gotten away with this for so long? How had he managed to keep each family a secret from each other as well as everyone else? In this day and age, with cell phones and e-mail and the Internet, how had he continued to keep his two lives separate?

She stared into space for a long time. It was only when a squirrel scampered across the path, startling the pigeons that were scavenging for food, that she was jerked out of her painful thoughts and she once more picked up the letter to finish reading it.

The letter ended with contact information for both Glynnis and her twin brother Gregg. Sabrina was startled to see that they lived only a couple of hours away, just north of Columbus. Somehow she'd envisioned her father's second life as taking place far from Rockwell.

Maybe you would prefer going to Gregg and telling him the truth and letting him break the news to Glynnis. Yes, this might be the best way.

Sabrina, please tell your mother that I am sorry about the scandal this will cause. I know how much her position in the town and her social circle matters to her.

Dear heaven, Sabrina thought. Even worse than confronting her father's other family would be breaking this news to her mother, for Sabrina had no illusions about Isabel's reaction. Her mother might not have loved her father the way Sabrina did, but she cared very much about her reputation. In fact, her standing in the town was probably the most important thing in her life. She would be devastated.

I am so sorry for the hurt I know you are feeling. Hurting you is the last thing I ever wanted to happen.

Although all Sabrina wanted to do was tear up the letter and put the whole nasty business out of her mind, she knew she couldn't do that. Those two small children—her half brother and half sister—were blameless in this affair. And now that she was over the initial shock, she had to admit, she was curious. What kind of woman was this Glynnis? Young and sexy, Sabrina imagined in disgust. Probably a curvy blonde with a Marilyn Monroe voice.

Daddy, how could you do this to us?

The pain she'd tried to quell hit her then, so swift and hard it was like a kick in the stomach. Her father said he loved her, but if he'd *really* loved her, he could not have done this awful thing. Marrying this, this Glynnis person, was a betrayal of everything he'd stood for.

Blindly she shoved the envelope into her handbag and stood. As she started on the path leading to the parking lot and her car, clouds moved across the sun, plunging the afternoon into darkness.

A darkness that was echoed in her heart.

Sabrina drove straight back to Leland Fox's office. She could see by the expression on his face that he had known the contents of the letter.

"How long have you known?" she asked.

"About six months."

Sabrina couldn't imagine why he had kept her father's secret. Leland and Isabel had grown up together. He had always been more her friend than Ben's. You'd think he'd have felt more loyalty toward her. She glared at him. But as quickly as her anger had come, it disappeared. None of this was Leland's fault.

"What are you going to do?" he asked. His eyes were kind.

"I guess I have no choice. I'll have to go see this woman and tell her about Dad's death."

He nodded sympathetically. "When you return, I'll help you break the news to your mother."

"You think I should wait before telling her?"

"There's no hurry, is there?"

Sabrina looked down at her lap. Leland was right. There was no hurry. Nothing would change whether she told her mother today or two weeks from now. In fact, it would be easier to wait until her mother was feeling stronger and over the shock of her father's death. She looked up, meeting Leland's eyes. "No, there's no hurry. And I'd be grateful for your help when I tell my mother."

Because she needed some time before facing her mother, Sabrina stopped at the office of *The Rockwell Record* on the way home.

Johnny Fiore, the sports editor who also handled school news and obituaries, looked up from his desk as she entered the newsroom. "Sabrina, how are you?" He stood up to give her a hug.

"I'm okay."

"We didn't expect you back till next week."

"I'm not here to work. I just stopped in to see how everything's going."

"She thinks we can't do without her," Kelsey Finnegan, the lifestyle/society/entertainment editor said, grinning at Sabrina.

"We can't. Things are falling apart without you here." This came from Vicki Barrows, the office manager/bookkeeper.

Sabrina smiled. She knew they were trying to lift

her spirits, and for a moment, they had. "I just want to take a look at my calendar, then I've got to go, but I'll be here on Monday."

As she sat at her desk surrounded by familiar things, she felt herself growing calmer. Because she'd said she was going to, she checked her calendar and saw that she'd set up an appointment with one of their suppliers for the next morning. She buzzed for Vicki. "You'll have to cancel tomorrow's appointment with Jake Evans. Tell him I'll call him to reschedule next week."

"Will do. Anything else?"

"Maybe you could ask Bert to cover the city council meeting." The Rockwell political scene was an area Sabrina had refused to give up, even as managerial responsibilities had pushed aside all other reporting duties.

"Sure thing."

"How's the ad count look?" Like most newspapers, advertising revenue dictated *The Record*'s size and provided most of its operating funds.

"As of the same date last year, we're up twenty-two percent."

Sabrina felt a surge of pride. They were having a banner year, due in large part to the hard work of Jan Kellogg, the new advertising manager Sabrina had hired in March.

Once all work-related details were taken care of, Sabrina logged on to the Internet and researched the town of Ivy, where Gregg Antonelli and his sister lived, and was pleased to discover a well-known chain motel located nearby. After making a reservation for the following night, Sabrina left the office and headed home.

On the way, all her worries came flooding back. How was she going to get through the rest of the day and all the ones to follow without raising her mother's suspicions? Although, since her accident, Sabrina's mother had been pretty self-involved, she was still fairly astute when it came to Sabrina and her emotions.

It was even harder than Sabrina had imagined to spend the afternoon and evening in her mother's company without giving away her state of turmoil, but somehow she managed. She and her mother and aunt had lunch together, then Irene suggested Isabel might like to take a nap. "I know I would," her aunt said.

To Sabrina's relief, her mother agreed. While her mother and aunt rested, Sabrina kept her thoughts under control by spending the afternoon at the piano. Music had always been her escape, and today was no exception. She played all her old favorites—Chopin, Beethoven, Bach, Schubert, with a sprinkling of Scott Joplin thrown in.

That night, Sabrina was extremely grateful for her aunt's presence at dinner. Irene kept the conversational ball rolling, something Sabrina knew she would not have been able to do if Irene hadn't been there.

Toward the end of the meal, Sabrina said as casually as she could, "Mom, tomorrow I have to go to Columbus to research a story."

Isabel stared at her. "So soon? Can't someone else do it?"

"No, I'm afraid not. This man…he's a whistle blower…" Oh, God, she hated lying. "And he only agreed to talk to me. It's really important or I wouldn't go. But you'll be okay. Aunt Irene and Florence are both here. And I'll only be gone one day."

Her mother looked as if she wanted to protest some more, but Irene forestalled her by saying, "It'll be good for Sabrina to get away, Isabel. And it'll give *us* a chance to go through Ben's clothes. You *did* say you wanted me to help you do that before I leave."

Isabel nodded reluctantly.

Sabrina smiled at her aunt, who reached over and patted her hand.

The following morning, Sabrina was on her way by eight. By eleven, she was pulling her Expedition into the parking lot of the motel. Luckily they had a room ready for her. After unpacking her few things, Sabrina sat on the side of the bed and reached for the phone. Her father's contact information for Gregg Antonelli was at his place of business—an Italian restaurant that he owned. Taking a deep breath, Sabrina punched in the numbers.

* * *

Gregg Antonelli told himself not to lose his temper, but there were times when Joe Ruggerio, his chef, tried Gregg's patience to the point where he'd like nothing better than to tell Joe to take a hike. Joe was the best chef Gregg had ever had, yet sometimes the problems he created simply didn't seem worth the benefits. Today was one of those days.

Gregg counted to ten. "Look, Joe, this has got to stop. Billy's a hard worker. I don't want to lose him."

The expression on Joe's florid face could only be described as a smirk.

Gregg's jaw hardened. "I mean it. I want you to give me your word you'll quit riding him."

"Hey, if he can't take the heat, he should get out of the kitchen!" Enamored of his own joke, Joe grinned and winked at Pedro, their dishwasher and Joe's lackey.

Gregg was about to say something he'd probably regret when Lisa, the head of the wait staff, entered the kitchen.

"Gregg, phone call for you," she said.

Saved by the bell, he thought, for if he'd given vent to his feelings, he wouldn't have had to fire Joe. The temperamental chef would have walked out. That was the crux of the problem. Great chefs were difficult to find, especially when you couldn't afford to pay top dollar, and Joe knew it.

Suppressing a tired sigh, Gregg headed for his minuscule office and punched the blinking line. "Gregg Antonelli."

"Um, yes. Mr. Antonelli?"

Gregg didn't recognize the female voice. "Yes," he said patiently. "This is Gregg Antonelli. How can I help you, ma'am?"

"Mr. Antonelli, my name is Sabrina March."

Gregg waited. The name meant nothing to him.

"I'm a, um, relative of Ben Arthur, who gave me your name. I know you don't know me, but it's very important that I talk to you about some urgent business. I'm only here in town for one day and was hoping we could meet this afternoon or evening."

Gregg frowned. He hadn't been aware that his sister's husband had any relatives. In fact, if he remembered correctly, Ben had specifically said he had no close family to speak of. So who the hell *was* this woman and what could she possibly want?

"If Ben gave you my name and this number, then you know I own a restaurant. I'll be tied up until at least ten-thirty tonight. But if you don't mind coming here, say, between eight-thirty and nine, I could meet with you then. That's when business begins to slow down, and if you like, we could have a late dinner together while we talk."

"Thank you. That sounds fine. Could you give me directions from the Comfort Inn?"

After they'd hung up, Gregg sat at his desk for a long moment. This woman must be on the up-and-up. How else would she know about him and his relationship to Glynnis? But what possible business could she have? Gregg wished he could talk to Ben before meeting with her, but Ben was away on one of his numerous trips and wasn't due back for another three days. Gregg supposed he could try to raise Ben on his cell phone. Quickly he looked up the number and called it, but all it yielded was Ben's voice mail.

"Hey, Ben, this is Gregg. If you get this message before eight tonight, give me a call. It's important."

Gregg wondered if he should call Glynnis next and see if she had any clue as to who this woman could be, but for some reason, he hesitated to do so. For one thing, his sister was a worrier. For another, his niece was suffering with an ear infection and Glynnis hadn't been getting a whole lot of sleep the past few days. For all he knew, she was napping along with the kids.

It was always tough on her when Ben was traveling, which was most of the time. Gregg's frown deepened. He had not been happy when Glynnis married Ben. Even if the man hadn't been nearly twenty years older than his sister, his frequent absences and his tendency to want to keep Glynnis to himself would have been enough to turn Gregg off. He'd always believed his sister could have done much better, but ever since she'd married Ben she'd seemed happy, so Gregg had kept his opinions to himself. He remembered only too well what had happened the last time he'd meddled in her love life.

Throughout the day, Gregg found himself thinking of the upcoming meeting whenever there was any kind of break in the action. Not that there were many. Antonelli's had always been popular with the lunch crowd, but for the past year—ever since a big computer software company had relocated its offices in the office complex a half mile down the road—they'd had a packed house every weekday.

When it finally slowed around two in the afternoon, the kitchen staff had all they could do to prepare for the evening meal, which started as early as five. In the afternoons, Gregg usually helped out in the kitchen because it wasn't only good chefs that were hard to come by. It was hard to find good help, period.

Today he worked on the salad line, cutting carrots and onions, which Maggie, the sous-chef, added to the torn pieces of romaine lettuce she'd arranged on the salad plates. They usually tried to plate at least fifty salads for the evening. Anything left over could be used at lunch the next day. A couple of sliced tomatoes would be added to the salads just before serving, because they did best if they weren't cut beforehand. There was nothing Gregg hated more than cold, mushy tomatoes on a salad.

In fact, he wouldn't tolerate that kind of sloppiness in his restaurant. He took pride in the fact that at Antonelli's they used the best and freshest possible ingredients available and that their salads had been given a high rating from the food editor of the local newspaper.

People who knew nothing about the restaurant business thought it was glamorous. Gregg himself had thought the same thing before he'd actually worked in one. There was nothing glamorous about it at all. It was extremely hard work, and half the startups didn't survive. Antonelli's had had a couple of rough years—years in which Gregg wasn't sure he'd make it, either—but a combination of hard work, informed planning, consistently good food, and luck had pulled him through.

Now Antonelli's was thriving.

But its success had come at a personal cost to Gregg. As always, when his thoughts turned to Lynn, his former fiancée, he felt a twinge of regret. They'd dated a couple of years and had been engaged another eighteen months before she'd called it quits a year ago. She'd said she could deal with a rival if the rival was female, but there was no way she was going to spend the rest of her life competing with a restaurant for his time and attention.

Gregg hadn't tried to change her mind. He'd loved Lynn, yes, but not enough to give up the business he'd worked so hard to build.

Not enough. Those were the key words, he guessed. At least that's what Glynnis had said.

"Hey, boss, you gonna work or you gonna daydream?" Maggie said, poking him.

Gregg blinked, then grinned. "Sorry." He began

to stack the salads on racks that would slide into one of the big refrigerators.

After that, the day passed quickly. So quickly that before Gregg knew it, it was eight o'clock. He alerted Janine, their evening hostess, that he was expecting a guest and asked her to buzz him in his office when the March woman arrived.

On the dot of eight-thirty, Janine said his visitor was there.

Too curious to wait, Gregg abandoned the supply order he'd been working on and walked out front. He saw the woman immediately. Janine had seated her in one of the alcoves, as Gregg had requested. The woman hadn't seen him yet; she was looking out the window, so he had a chance to study her for a few moments.

She was pretty and younger than she'd sounded on the phone—probably in her middle twenties. She wore her dark, chin-length hair swept back from her face and caught up in the back with some kind of silver clip. She was dressed simply, in black slacks and a wine-colored sweater. A black leather jacket was draped across the back of her chair.

As he got closer, she turned, and their eyes met. Hers were large and gray—beautiful eyes, he thought—and filled with an emotion he couldn't identify. He frowned. What was it? Concern? Uncertainty? Fear? Whatever it was, it only reinforced his own uneasiness over the reason for her appearance in Ivy.

"Miss March? I'm Gregg Antonelli." He held out his hand, and she took it. Her hand felt cool, and her handshake was firm.

"Hi. Thank you for seeing me on such short notice."

He liked her voice. It was much softer than it had seemed on the phone. Gregg sat down across from her and beckoned to Chris, who waited on this section. "Would you like a glass of wine?"

"I don't think so, thank you."

"What about dinner? You *were* still planning to eat with me?"

"Yes, I'd love to." She looked around. "This is a very nice restaurant."

"Thanks. We've done well."

Picking up the menu, she studied it for a moment, then said, "What do you recommend?"

"Depends what you like. Pasta? Chicken? Veal?"

She put the menu down and for the first time, she smiled. "I'm a pasta person."

"Then I recommend the combination ravioli and tortellini. That's our specialty. My personal preference is the marinara sauce, but we do offer it with a cheese sauce, if you'd prefer that."

"That sounds good. With the marinara sauce."

Gregg turned to Chris. "We'll both have the ravioli and tortellini, and I'll have a glass of the house Chianti. And the lady will have...?"

"Iced tea, please."

Within moments Chris had brought them a basket

of warm focaccia bread and a plate of seasoned olive oil for dipping, followed by their drinks. All the while he was serving them, Gregg studied Sabrina March. She was a small woman, with narrow wrists and slender arms. He'd bet, standing, she wouldn't reach five feet four inches. She had a small, heart-shaped face which, along with those expressive gray eyes, made her seem vulnerable, yet her voice and mannerisms and the way she met his gaze squarely suggested self-confidence. It was an intriguing mix that he found especially attractive.

When Chris left them to get their salads, Gregg said, "Tell me, Miss March, just how are you related to Ben?"

She reached for a piece of bread, hesitated, then said, "I'd rather explain why I'm here first."

Gregg tensed at the evasive answer, certain now that he wasn't going to like what she had to say.

"First of all, please call me Sabrina."

"All right, if you'll call me Gregg."

She put down her piece of bread. Leaning forward, she fixed those big eyes on him. "I just want you to know that I hate having to bring you this kind of news."

"What news?"

She spoke slowly. "The man you know as Ben Arthur is dead. He died last Thursday."

"*What?*" Gregg stared at her. "That can't be true."

"I'm sorry. I'm afraid it *is* true."

"And just what do you mean by *the man you know as Ben Arthur?*"

"His…his name is really Ben March. Benjamin Arthur March."

"Look, I don't know what you're trying to pull—"

"I'm not trying to pull anything," she cried. "I'm telling you the truth."

She reached for her handbag and pulled out a wallet. Removing two laminated cards, she handed them to him. They were both Ohio driver's licenses. Her picture was on the first card. Sabrina Isabel March. An address in Rockwell, Ohio. And Ben's picture was on the second. Benjamin Arthur March. With another Rockwell address.

Gregg felt as if someone had kicked him in the stomach. What the hell was going on here?

"Mr. Antonelli…Gregg," she continued softly, "I'm so sorry." She sighed deeply. "You asked me how I'm related to…Ben. Ben March is…was…my father."

"Your father," he said dully.

"Yes."

"But—"

"I know, he never said anything about having a daughter. Obviously, there were a lot of things he didn't tell you."

Gregg didn't know what to think. "I don't understand. Why didn't he tell us about you? I mean, he told my sister he was divorced. And why use a different name? It doesn't make any sense.''

''I know. The thing is, when my father met your sister, he wasn't divorced. He was still married. To my mother.''

As she continued to explain, Gregg learned that Ben had *never* divorced his wife. That his wife…Sabrina's mother…still lived. That his marriage to Glynnis was not valid. That Ben was a bigamist.

Gregg was speechless. How was he going to tell Glynnis? It would have been hard enough to tell her Ben was dead, but this! This would kill her. Shock gave way to fury as the truth finally sank in. Damn Ben. Damn his very soul. Glynnis didn't deserve this. Gregg hoped Ben burned in hell.

''I'm so sorry,'' Sabrina said again. ''I know how you feel, because I feel the same way. I just couldn't believe it when I read my dad's letter.''

''That's how you found out? Through a letter?'' Gregg asked. He didn't try to disguise his scorn.

''Yes. He'd given the letter to our attorney with instructions to give it to me in the event of his death.''

''How *did* he die?'' At this point, Gregg didn't really care, but he knew Glynnis would want to know.

''He had a heart attack. We…we were walking in the park in the town where…where we live…and he collapsed. The emergency personnel tried to save him, but it was too late.'' Her eyes glistened.

Oh, hell. He hoped she wasn't going to cry. He had enough to handle right now without a weepy woman on his hands. But though he told himself this, he felt bad. She was as much a victim in this mess as Glynnis was.

Then their food arrived, and they didn't talk until Chris had finished serving them and walked away. By then she'd gotten herself under control again.

"Does your mother know about this?" Gregg asked.

"No. I haven't told her yet." She looked away. "It's going to be one of the hardest things I'll ever have to do."

Yeah. He knew exactly what she meant.

She picked up her fork. Speared a tortellini. Then she put the fork down again. "I'm sorry. The food looks wonderful, but I no longer have any appetite."

"I know." Gregg's appetite had gone south, too. "But you need to eat. Come on."

She shook her head. "I can't. I'm sorry. Is…is there anything else you'd like to ask me?"

"Nothing I can think of right now."

"Well, if you do think of something…" She reached for her handbag again. This time she withdrew a business card. "That's where I work. You can call me there anytime. If I'm not in, call my cell phone number."

After she left, Gregg debated whether to go and see Glynnis immediately or wait until morning to break the news. He decided to wait. He might as well allow his sister to have one more peaceful night before she had to find out the sordid truth.

Besides, he couldn't face telling her tonight. He hadn't completely digested the news himself, plus he was tired. It had been a long and busy day.

And Glynnis was going to need him to be strong. Best to get a good night's sleep himself so he wouldn't let her down when she needed him most.

Chapter Three

Sabrina couldn't get Gregg Antonelli out of her mind. She hadn't expected to like him; she certainly hadn't expected to sympathize with him, but she had. She did.

He had a terrible job in front of him. It wouldn't be easy telling his sister what he'd learned. Yet although Sabrina had only met the man tonight, she could tell he was equal to the task. Strength and confidence were written all over him. He was the type of man who would face any crisis head-on. He was also the type of man women gravitated toward.

Sabrina wondered if he was involved with anyone. For some reason, she didn't think he was married. Why, she couldn't have said. It was just a feeling she had. Besides, he hadn't been wearing a wedding ring. Funny how she'd noticed.

Oh, come on, admit it. You were attracted to him. Of course you noticed.

It was discomfiting to admit it, because under the circumstances, her reaction to Gregg Antonelli was totally inappropriate.

Forget about him, she told herself. He'll do what he has to do, and you'll do what you have to do, and you'll probably never see him again.

Deliberately, she turned her thoughts to her mother and the best way to approach the coming ordeal.

The next morning, Gregg rose early. He showered and shaved, drank his coffee, then picked up the phone. Glynnis was a stay-at-home mother, but she was a morning person, so even though it was only seven-thirty, Gregg knew she'd be up. In this they were alike.

Truth was, in most things they were alike. The only thing noticeably different about them was their appearance. He looked like their father; she resembled their mother. Gregg's hair was a medium brown. Her hair was a reddish-blond. His eyes were blue, hers were hazel. They were both tall, but there the physical similarity ended.

The surface differences meant nothing, though. They had always been close, always been able to tell what the other was feeling without words.

They'd faced tough stuff before. The death of their

parents had been especially difficult. But they'd never faced anything like this. This was the worst.

Quit stalling. He punched in the code for her home. It rang twice.

"Good morning," she said.

"Good morning."

"I love this caller ID."

In the background he could hear the children. "Kids are up already, huh?"

"Oh, yes. Lately they've been getting up before seven."

"Guess they're going to be morning people, too."

She chuckled. "Until they hit their teens, anyway. So, bro, what's on your mind so early this morning?"

"I was thinking maybe you'd feed me breakfast."

"Sure. The kids'll love to see their Uncle Gregg. Well, I will, too. What would you like? Waffles? Scrambled eggs and biscuits?"

"Waffles sounds good."

"Waffles it is, then. Are you coming now?"

"Be there in fifteen minutes."

Driving over to Glynnis's house, Gregg couldn't stop thinking about what was going to happen to his sister now. With two little kids to raise on her own, her life wouldn't be easy. At least she wouldn't be penniless. Gregg knew Ben had taken out an insurance policy shortly after they were married. But it wasn't a huge policy. If she had to live on it, it wouldn't last five years.

He frowned as a thought struck him.

What if the insurance company wouldn't honor the policy because her marriage to Ben wasn't legal? Could they do that?

No. He was sure they couldn't. Anyone could be the beneficiary of an insurance policy. You didn't even have to be related to the person who'd died.

She'd get the money.

And then another thought left him cold. What name had Ben used on the policy? His real one? Or the name he used to marry Glynnis? Gregg made a mental note to call his lawyer as soon as he got back to the restaurant. He had a feeling they were going to need him.

Even if the insurance thing was okay, Glynnis would still have to go back to work a lot sooner than she'd expected. Gregg knew she'd been planning to teach again when Olivia, her youngest, started school. But Olivia was barely two years old. It was going to be hard for Glynnis to leave her. Michael was five and more independent. He had started kindergarten this year, so day care afterward probably wouldn't faze him.

Briefly Gregg wondered if Ben had left Glynnis anything else. He'd always been vague about his business affairs, and since he and Gregg had not been close, Gregg wasn't sure what Ben's financial situation had been. There'd always seemed to be plenty of money, though, and now that Gregg knew the truth of Ben's situation, he realized Ben must have been fairly well-off if he was supporting two households.

Had he been, though?

Or was Sabrina's mother a successful career woman herself? *Damn.* Why hadn't he asked Sabrina more questions last night? He didn't even know if she was Ben's only other child. For all Gregg knew she could have brothers and sisters.

Jeez. What a mess.

Furious again, he pounded the steering wheel. What had possessed Ben to do what he had? Even though Gregg hadn't been thrilled by the marriage, he could have sworn Ben really loved Glynnis. Why hadn't he just divorced Sabrina's mother? Why the lies that were going to cause so many people so much pain?

But there were no answers to these questions, because the only person who knew the answers was dead. Now all that was left to do was clean up the mess Ben had left behind.

When Sabrina got back to Rockwell, she decided to go to her apartment rather than straight back to her parents' home—no—she had to quit thinking of it as her parents' home. It was now solely her mother's home.

At the realization, a fresh wave of sadness flooded her. No matter how hurt she was by her father's duplicity, nothing changed the fact that she had loved him. She would always love him, no matter what he'd done. And she knew he had felt the same way about her.

He would have forgiven me anything, and I need to forgive him.

Pulling into the covered parking slot behind her back door, she could feel some of the stress of the past few days begin to lessen. Her apartment always had this effect on her. From the moment she'd first seen it, she'd loved it. The apartment was located in a small complex near Rockwell University—on the opposite side of town from where her parents lived. Typical of areas around colleges, the neighborhood was trendy and popular with the younger residents of Rockwell.

Sabrina especially loved that she could walk to neighborhood shops and restaurants if she wanted to. One street over from hers had a movie theater, a bookstore, a coffee shop and a bakery. On weekend mornings, she loved to walk over to the bakery and buy fresh bagels or crusty rolls, then take them home to enjoy with a latte purchased from the coffee shop.

Her mother had fought Sabrina's moving out of the family home, insisting there was plenty of room and it was ridiculous for her to pay rent when she practically had her own suite and all the privacy she could want right there. "It makes no sense at all."

But Sabrina had been firm, saying, "Mother, I'm twenty-four years old. I've been out of college for nearly two years. It's time to cut the cord."

Her father had backed her up. "Everyone needs

their own space, Isabel. We can't keep Sabrina a child forever.''

That had been four years ago, and Sabrina had never been sorry she'd moved. Sure, it had been nice to have Florence waiting on her, doing her laundry, not having to buy food or pay rent, but those luxuries didn't compare to the thrill of having her own place and the satisfaction of paying her own way.

Entering her apartment, she even breathed easier. It smelled a bit musty from being shut up for more than a week, and it needed cleaning, but it was hers. Every stick of furniture was there because she'd chosen it and she'd paid for it. She had taken nothing from the family home, even though her mother had offered all the furniture in her bedroom and adjoining sitting room.

Isabel had turned up her nose at the inexpensive furniture and discount house accessories Sabrina had purchased, but Sabrina didn't care. All the antiques and valuable objets d'art that filled the March home hadn't been enough to make her mother happy. They certainly didn't tempt Sabrina if it meant giving up her independence.

It was bad enough, she thought, that she was trapped in a job that no longer fulfilled her and shackled by duties and responsibilities she hadn't asked for. Her apartment was her oasis, the only place where she felt at peace.

Sabrina had stopped at the mailboxes on her way into the complex, and now she sorted through her mail. There was nothing urgent—a few bills, a few pieces of junk mail and her newest copy of *Vanity Fair*.

She then headed for her bedroom. After changing clothes and unpacking, she put a load of laundry in the washer, opened some windows to air the place out, and cleaned the refrigerator, getting rid of anything that looked as if it might be past its prime.

She debated calling the paper, then decided there was no reason to. If anything urgent came up, they would call her. Finally she could stall no longer and knew she had to decide what she was going to do when she finally did go to her mother's.

Should she tell her mother everything today?

Or should she wait?

It was difficult for Gregg to pretend this was a normal visit with Glynnis and the children, but somehow he managed it while Michael was still there. But once Michael's car pool came and he was off to kindergarten and Olivia was almost finished eating her breakfast, Gregg knew he could no longer put off telling Glynnis the bad news.

"There's something I need to talk to you about." He glanced over at Olivia, who had just stuffed a last piece of waffle and cut-up strawberry into her mouth. "Think you could set her up with a video in the playroom?"

Glynnis smiled. "Sure." Turning to her daughter,

she said, "Livvy, pumpkin, would you like to watch Dumbo?"

"Dumbo, Dumbo!" Olivia shouted, her hazel eyes—a mirror of her mother's—shining.

She grinned at Gregg, who grinned back. His niece could always make him smile.

"I guess her earache is gone," Glynnis said in wry amusement. "She's gone back to her normal tone of voice. Loud."

Gregg chuckled.

Once Glynnis had cleaned syrup off Olivia's face and hands, Gregg took his niece out of her high chair and carried her into the playroom, which was on the other side of the kitchen. The builder had intended it to be a sunroom, but it made a perfect play area for the kids, with lots of light and proximity to the place where their mother spent a good portion of her time.

"I can be working in the kitchen and still keep a close eye on them," she'd said happily. In fact, she'd admitted later that the sunroom was the top selling point when it came to making a decision about buying the house.

Once Olivia, surrounded by her stuffed animals, was settled on the floor in front of the TV, Gregg and Glynnis walked back into the kitchen, and she poured them each a fresh cup of coffee.

"Now, what's on your mind?" she said, settling herself at the kitchen table. She reached for the sugar bowl and added two heaping teaspoons to her coffee. Sugar in her coffee was one of her few indulgences.

His heart ached at the unsuspecting smile on his sister's face. She probably thought he had a problem at the restaurant, the kind of thing he usually wanted to discuss with her.

Girding himself, he made his voice gentle. "I've got some bad news, Glynnie. You're going to have to be strong."

The smile on her face slowly faded. She put her coffee cup down. "What is it?"

Reaching across the table, he took her hand. "There's no easy way to tell you this." The fear in her eyes made Gregg wish he could be anywhere else but there. "Ben is dead, Glynnie."

Her hand jerked, but he held fast. She shook her head. "That…that can't be. Wh-why would you say such a thing?"

"I'm so sorry. I wish it wasn't true, but I'm afraid it is."

"No." She kept shaking her head. "No."

"Glynnie, listen to me. It's true. Ben had a heart attack last Thursday, and he died almost immediately."

"Last *Thursday!* But…but *where?*" she cried. "How? I-I don't understand. It can't be true. Someone would have called me. It's a mistake. It *has* to be. He's not dead. Don't you *see?* Someone would have *called* me, Gregg!" Her eyes pleaded with him to say it was all a big mix-up. "It's true I haven't heard from him, but that's because he's abroad. This is just a mistake."

"I'm sorry. It's not a mistake. Ben is dead."

Suddenly she just dissolved. Her face crumpled, and tears welled in her eyes. "No," she wailed. "No, no, no, no..."

Gregg wanted to cry himself. He got up and took her into his arms. Her body shook with sobs. From the playroom came the sounds of happy music and Olivia's laughter.

When Glynnis finally calmed, he sat her down again and pulled his chair close to hers.

"How...how did you find out?" she asked tonelessly. "Did someone from the company he was working for call you or was it the Greek authorities? Are they shipping his body home?"

Gregg took her hand again. "No, it was nothing like that. Ben didn't die in Greece. He died right here in Ohio."

"Here in *Ohio?*"

"Yes. Look, I need to back up and start at the beginning. Okay?"

She nodded miserably.

If Gregg could have spared her this...but he couldn't. He had to tell her everything. "Yesterday I got a call at work..."

As he talked, telling her about Sabrina, what she'd said, how she'd come to the restaurant last night, and what she'd revealed to him, he saw a host of emotions play across his sister's face and in her eyes. Shock, disbelief, denial, anger and lastly, an almost tranquil acceptance.

She sat unmoving, staring sightlessly into space, silent for so long Gregg became uneasy.

Finally she stirred. "Poor Ben," she said softly.

"Poor *Ben?*"

"He must have felt so desperate." Glynnis's eyes, swimming with tears, met his. "He loved me, Gregg. I'm as sure of that as I am of anything in my life. He would never purposely have hurt me. For him to be driven to something like this…obviously he felt he had no choice."

Gregg wanted to tell her she was crazy to be defending him, but something about the look on her face stopped him. Ah, hell, he thought. If it made her feel better to think well of Ben, what harm was there in that?

"I know what you're thinking. But I'm right, I know I am. Ben would never have done what he did if he wasn't desperate."

"Right now, his reasons don't matter. What matters is the future. We need to talk about what you're going to do. You'll have to—"

"Does his…his other wife know?"

"She didn't as of last night, but I think Ben's daughter was going to tell her today." This was strictly guesswork on Gregg's part, for Sabrina had not said anything other than that her mother didn't know the situation.

Glynnis wiped away her tears with her hands. "Do you know anything about her? The other wife?"

"No. I didn't ask."

"What about his daughter? What was she like? Did she look like Ben?"

"Not really. She has dark hair like he did, but she's little and has gray eyes. She must look like her mother."

"I—I can't get over it. Michael and Olivia have a sister." This was said with wonder.

"Half sister."

Her gaze shot to his. "You hate Ben, don't you?"

"No. I don't hate him." This was true. The emotion Gregg felt was stronger than hate, but there was no sense in telling her this and making her feel worse. "I hate what he did. I hate what this is doing to you. And what it's going to do to the kids."

She bowed her head. "I'm going to miss him so much."

He could see how hard she was trying to keep herself under control. Ashamed of himself, he softened his voice. "Ah, Glynnie. You know I'll do everything I can to make this easier—"

"I want to talk to her. Meet her."

"Who? Sabrina?"

"Yes."

"I'm not sure that's a good idea."

"I don't care. I want to see her. I need to see her."

When he still hesitated, she said, "Please, Gregg. Will you call her?"

He thought about the business card he'd left on his dresser. And he thought about how much he had liked Sabrina March.

He sighed. "All right, Glynnie. If it means that much to you, I'll call her later today."

After giving it much thought, Sabrina decided the easiest and kindest way she could break the news to her mother was to simply give her the letter her father had written. Taking the letter out again, she re-read it and abruptly changed her mind. Better not to let her mother see the things her father had said about Glynnis and the children.

There's not going to be an easy way out for you. You're going to have to tell her yourself.

Once the decision was made, she realized there was no point in putting off the inevitable, so she called Leland Fox and asked him to meet her at her mother's house at four o'clock.

Then she called her mother.

"Where are you?" There was a petulant note in her mother's voice. "I thought you'd be back hours ago."

"I did get back earlier, but I had some things that needed to be taken care of here at the apartment, and since I knew Aunt Irene was there with you..." Sabrina let her voice trail off and told herself not to get irritated. Her mother was under a lot of stress.

"You *are* going to be here for dinner, aren't you? I told Florence you were."

"Yes, of course, I am. In fact, I'll be there in about an hour."

A few minutes before four, Sabrina pulled into the

driveway of the family home. She'd barely gotten the door open and was just stepping out of the car when Leland pulled in behind her.

"I'm dreading this," he said. He looked awful. There were dark circles under his eyes as if he hadn't been sleeping well.

"Me, too." Sabrina felt sorry for him. This wasn't his problem. But she was terribly grateful for his presence. She had no idea how her mother was going to react, and Leland's presence always had a calming effect.

"Leland! We didn't know you were coming over," Sabrina's aunt said as they walked into the foyer. She looked bright and cheerful in a pink cashmere sweater set and dark wool skirt, but her smile faded at the expressions on their faces.

"Hello, Irene." Leland smiled and gave her a hug. "How're you holding up?"

"Oh, I'm all right." Her voice lowered. "But there's something's wrong, isn't there?" She looked worriedly from him to Sabrina.

Sabrina nodded grimly. "Yes. Where's Mom?"

"In the sunroom. Do...do you want me to make myself scarce?"

"No, there's something we have to tell her, but I think it's a good idea for you to be there, too. We might need you."

Sabrina's mother, who was leafing through a magazine, looked up as the three of them entered the

room. "Hello, Leland. I thought I heard your voice."
A rare smile softened her features.

"Hello, Isabel. How are you, my dear?" He bent
down and kissed her.

"I'm fine."

Sabrina's heart ached. "Mom," she began.
"We—"

"Leland, would you like something to drink?" Isabel interrupted.

He shook his head and sat on one of the rattan
armchairs nearest to her. He reached for her hand.
She gave him a puzzled look but didn't try to pull
away.

"Mother," Sabrina started again. "I asked Leland
to come over today because there's something we
need to tell you."

Isabel looked at him with raised eyebrows.
"Something about the will?"

"No, not about the will," Leland said.

"It's... Dad left a letter for me in Leland's safekeeping," Sabrina said. "Leland gave it to me the
day before yesterday."

The next few minutes were excruciating for Sabrina as she once more recounted the contents of the
letter.

Both her mother and her aunt gasped almost simultaneously when Sabrina got to the part about Ben
marrying another woman.

"He *what?*" her mother exclaimed. "Is this a
joke?" She directed this last question to Leland.

"No, Isabel, I'm afraid it's no joke."

"I don't believe you."

"Mom..." Sabrina said.

"Isabel, my dear," Leland said, "I know you don't want to believe it, but Sabrina has told you the truth. Ben married another woman almost seven years ago."

Sabrina's mother stared at Leland. Sabrina knew the exact moment she reconciled herself to what had been said, because her face tightened into an ugly mask of fury. "That *bastard!*" she said through gritted teeth. "That son of a bitch!"

"Isabel!" Irene said.

Even Sabrina was shocked. Her mother never swore. She was fond of saying that those who used foul language were lazy and common.

"How could he *do* this to me! How could he humiliate me this way?" Furious tears ran down Isabel's face, and she yanked her hand from Leland's. Pounding her fists on the arms of her wheelchair, she spewed invectively. "If he wasn't already dead, I'd kill him myself! God *damn* him. I hope he burns in hell forever!"

Irene pulled her chair over to her sister's and tried to take her sister's hand.

But Sabrina's mother was having none of it. Her sobs had escalated into hysteria and she swatted away any gesture of comfort. Sabrina looked at Leland and her aunt helplessly. Her mother's reaction was even worse than Sabrina had imagined it would be, and Sabrina hadn't even gotten to the part about the other children Ben had fathered. Oh, God. What would her mother say to *that?* That would be the ultimate betrayal, because Sabrina knew her parents had wanted more children but had been unable to have them.

Finally Leland pulled Sabrina out into the hallway. "Call Doc Robinson. Tell him I said it's an emergency and he's needed here immediately."

Fortunately, Dr. Truman Robinson was an old family friend who asked no questions. Within thirty minutes, he was at the door. Although Sabrina's mother cried she didn't want anything, he insisted on giving her a shot, saying it would make her feel better. As soon as the sedative began to work, Irene said she'd take her sister upstairs where she could lie down.

Although Sabrina had wanted to get the entire thing over with today, she decided her aunt was right. Time enough to tell her mother about the children when she was over this first shock.

When they heard the elevator that had been installed after Isabel's accident begin its ascent to the second level of the house, the doctor looked at Sabrina. "What happened?"

Sabrina hesitated. She knew it was only a matter of time before people found out about all this because it was impossible to keep a secret of this magnitude in a small town. Still she hated to tell the doctor. On the other hand, he'd gone above and beyond what could be expected of him today, and in return, he deserved to know why he'd been called.

"You tell him," she said to Leland.

The doctor shook his head after Leland explained. "Poor Isabel."

"I'm sure the family would appreciate your not saying anything just yet," Leland said. "Give Isabel some time to come to grips with the situation."

"I won't say anything, period," Dr. Robinson said. "None of my business."

After he'd gone, Leland asked Sabrina if she'd like him to stay.

"No, it's okay. We can manage."

"Call me if you need me."

"We will."

The house was so quiet after he left, Sabrina wasn't sure she could stand it. She wanted, more than anything, to escape to her own apartment, but she knew that was a cowardly, selfish wish. When her mother awakened, she would need Sabrina.

Oh, God, Sabrina thought. *I'm not sure I'm up to the next few days.*

She knew once her mother's initial shock wore off, she would be coldly furious. And if she ever found out about Sabrina's role in this affair, she would be hurt beyond belief.

I must never let her know that I went to Ivy. Never. And I must never go there again.

Chapter Four

The next day, Gregg placed a call to the newspaper where Sabrina worked.

"I'm sorry," the young woman who answered the phone said, "there's been a death in the family, and Sabrina is out of the office. Can someone else help you?"

"No, thanks, it's personal."

"Well, if you'll leave your name and number, I'll give her the message."

"That's okay. I'll try her cell phone."

But when he called Sabrina's cell phone, he got her voice mail and had to be content with leaving her a message after all. He wondered if she would call him back.

It was nearly ten that night when Janine buzzed him to say Miss March was on the line for him.

"Sabrina?" He was smiling. "Thanks for calling back."

"I'm sorry I couldn't call sooner. Things are kind of rough around here right now, and I had to wait until my mother went to bed."

"You live with your mother?"

"No, I have my own place, but...well...I didn't tell you, but my mother is in a wheelchair. Sixteen years ago, she had a skiing accident that left her paralyzed from the waist down."

"Jeez, that's rough." Gregg's mind spun with this revelation. "Does she know? About my sister?"

She sighed. "Yes. I had to tell her in stages, but she knows everything now."

"I told my sister, too."

"How'd she take it?"

"Better than I would have," he said dryly.

"My mother became hysterical. I—I've never seen her like this before. She's always been so dignified. Even after her accident, she never fell apart. But this...this has just shattered her."

"It's got to be worse for her than anyone else."

She was silent for a long moment. "I hadn't thought of it that way, but I guess you're right."

"Are you going to be staying with her for a while?"

"I have to. It's hard, but my aunt—my mother's sister—is only going to be here until Wednesday. I guess whether I stay longer or not depends on how my mother is doing by then.''

He could hear the strain in her voice. This was tough on her. A lot tougher than it was on him. Especially since Glynnis had proved to be stronger than he had anticipated.

''I hate to add to your problems,'' he said after a bit. ''But my sister would really like to meet you and talk to you.'' When she didn't answer immediately, he was afraid she was going to say no. Disappointment pricked him, yet he understood why she might be hesitant. She owed nothing to Glynnis, and if she preferred not to have anything else to do with Glynnis or him, that was her prerogative.

Then she surprised him by saying, ''I want to meet her, too.''

''Great,'' he said eagerly. ''When? I'm assuming it's best for you to come here.''

''No question about that. But I don't know when I can manage it. With my aunt going home, there will be no one here except for our housekeeper. I'm sorry, but I just can't leave my mother alone right now. I've even had to put off going back to work.''

''Don't apologize. I understand.''

''I'll call you the end of next week and let you know how things are going, okay?'' As if to herself, she murmured, ''Maybe I can persuade my aunt to stay longer.''

''Great,'' he said again. ''I'll tell Glynnis. Oh, and there's one other thing. I, uh, hate to have to mention this, but Glynnis is going to need a copy of the death certificate.'' When she said nothing, he explained, ''For insurance purposes. Your father bought an insurance policy on himself after he married Glynnis.''

''Oh. Okay. I'll get her a copy.''

''It has to be a certified copy.''

''All right. That's no problem. I'll mail it to you.''

''You can just bring it when you come. And Sabrina?''

''Yes?''

Now it was his turn to hesitate. Then he thought, *What the hell. Go for it.* ''I know the circumstances aren't the best, but I'm looking forward to seeing you again.'' Once the words were out, he held his breath.

''I...'' Her voice softened. He could almost see her smile. ''Me, too.''

Gregg knew it was crazy, but he felt ridiculously happy when he hung up.

That night, Sabrina wrestled with her conscience. She knew, if she were wise, she'd call Gregg back in the morning and tell him she'd changed her mind, that she wasn't coming to Ivy again. If her mother ever found out about it, she would never forgive Sabrina. And Sabrina wouldn't blame her.

But in the morning her curiosity and desire to meet Glynnis and the children overrode her guilt, and she didn't do a thing.

Her mother was still extremely unstable emotionally. She would seem okay, then suddenly she would start crying. Sabrina's aunt did her best to calm Isabel, but even she gave up eventually. "Maybe it's best to let her get it all out of her system," she said. "After all, this has been a horrible thing to happen."

She shook her head. "I don't know, Sabrina. Your father didn't seem like the kind of person who would do something like this. If you and Leland hadn't assured me that all of this is true, I would never have believed it of him."

"I know." Sabrina was so grateful to her aunt, who hadn't even needed to be asked to stay longer. That morning she'd announced that her husband could get along without her for a couple more weeks, that they'd talked about it, and he'd urged her to stay.

Sabrina had thrown her arms around her aunt. "Thank you," she said. "Thank you."

"Oh, honey, I know this is hard on you. I wouldn't abandon you."

By Friday, Sabrina knew that even if she hadn't been planning a trip to Ivy, she would have had to get away. Somehow the news about her father had leaked out, and since then, the phone hadn't stopped ringing. The callers all expressed their shock and sympathy, but her mother didn't believe any of them.

"They're all *thrilled* this has happened to me," she said bitterly. "Well, if they think I'm going to cry and wail in front of them, they've got another think coming. I wouldn't give them the satisfaction."

Sabrina was glad to see her mother had rallied

enough to regain the fierce pride that had sustained her through many past problems.

Sabrina herself also received quite a few calls, but she felt those who called her really were sympathetic, especially the people she worked with at the paper and good friends like Casey, who cared about her.

"Oh, God, Sabrina, I'm so sorry," Casey said. "I know how tough this must be for you. How's your mother doing?"

"Oh, you know. She's mad as hell, but she's determined not to let anyone see her sweat."

"If you need me…"

"I know."

Leland, too, was a rock. He stopped by the house at least once every day, usually in the late afternoon. He'd stay an hour or two, having a cocktail with her mother and listening to anything she wanted to say. A couple of times he even stayed for dinner.

Sabrina wondered what Cecily, his wife, thought about all this. She and Isabel had never hit it off. Cecily wasn't from Rockwell, and Isabel had said more times than Sabrina could count, how Leland could have done much better for himself. Sometimes Sabrina suspected that maybe her mother had once had a thing for Leland and wondered what, if anything, had happened to cause them to marry other people.

On Sunday night, more than a week after Gregg had called her, she decided it was time to broach the subject of going back to work. So after dinner, while she and her aunt and mother were eating the apple pie Florence had made, Sabrina said, "Mom, I'm going back to work tomorrow."

"Already?"

"It's time."

Her mother pursed her lips, but she didn't say anything else. Sabrina's eyes met her aunt's, who nodded encouragingly.

I refuse to feel guilty, Sabrina thought.

Later, after her aunt and mother had gone up to bed, Sabrina phoned Antonelli's. When Gregg came on the line, she said, "I'll come on Wednesday and stay over that night."

"What time Wednesday?"

"I should get there about eleven in the morning."

"When you get in, call me at the restaurant. I'll come over to your hotel and pick you up."

"All right, that sounds good."

After she hung up, she called and made another motel reservation, then began to pack her belongings.

Tomorrow night, after work, she would be going home. And on Wednesday, she would see Gregg Antonelli again.

On Wednesday, Gregg waited impatiently for the phone call from Sabrina. He was glad Sabrina had decided to come, but he was apprehensive about the coming meeting. Glynnis had been hurt enough. If Sabrina should say or do anything to inflict additional pain on his sister, he'd have to get her out of there.

He didn't think Sabrina would intentionally hurt Glynnis—she hadn't seemed like that kind of person—but the whole situation was so loaded with pitfalls, she might hurt Glynnis without meaning to.

It was eleven-fifteen when the call finally came.

"You made it," he said.

"Yes, I'm here."

"Where shall I pick you up?"

"I'll be waiting out front. They didn't have a room ready for me yet, so I haven't checked in."

Before leaving, Gregg went into the kitchen. All seemed calm today. "I'm going to be out for a couple of hours. If you need me, page me." He looked at Joe, who ignored him.

"Things are fine," Maggie said.

Gregg wanted to say they'd better stay fine, but he didn't. No sense in baiting Joe.

Fifteen minutes later, he pulled into the parking lot of the motel. Sabrina was standing under the covered entrance, and when she saw him she waved. She looked great in jeans and a black turtleneck sweater under a short denim jacket. Today her hair was loose, and it framed her face in a mass of dark waves. Silver earrings and a matching bracelet gleamed from her ears and right wrist.

"I thought I'd just follow you," she said, walking over to his truck. "That way I'll have my car and won't have to bother you for a ride home."

"It's no bother."

"Are you sure?"

"Positive."

"Well, okay."

Once they were on their way, he said, "How was your trip?"

"Not bad. I'm not crazy about the interstate, but it was the fastest way to get here."

They didn't talk much after that, and Gregg finally realized she was probably just as tense as he was about today's meeting with Glynnis. That knowledge made him like her even more than he already did.

Suddenly he stopped worrying. He was a good judge of character, and he knew instinctively that Sabrina March would not hurt Glynnis.

If anything, the meeting of the two women might just help both of them heal.

Glynnis was nothing like Sabrina had thought she would be, although she should have known Gregg's twin wouldn't be what she'd first imagined when she'd realized her father had fallen in love with another woman. In fact, Sabrina hadn't been around Glynnis ten minutes when she knew exactly why her father had found it impossible to give her up.

Glynnis was the exact opposite of Sabrina's mother. Where Isabel was cool and patrician, Glynnis was warm and earthy. Where Isabel rarely let anyone see what she was really feeling, Glynnis was open and wore her emotions right out there in plain sight. And although both women were intelligent, Isabel's intelligence took the form of remarks that left the listener with no doubt that she knew she had a superior intellect, whereas Glynnis's showed itself in her common sense.

And, Sabrina admitted sadly, her mother had absolutely no sense of humor, whereas Glynnis, even in this tense and awkward situation, smiled and laughed often, even if the laughter was at her own expense.

Although Sabrina didn't want to, she liked Glynnis. She liked her a lot. In other circumstances, they could easily have been friends.

And when she said, just minutes after meeting Sabrina, "I am so sorry for the pain you and your mother have had to go through," every one of Sabrina's defenses were torn away, because she could see Glynnis was sincere.

And after all, Sabrina thought, none of this was Glynnis's fault. She didn't know Ben was married when she met him. She didn't purposely deceive anyone, as he had. She was as much a victim of this mess as Sabrina's mother. Maybe even more so, because she'd been left with two small children to raise, and Isabel had no one but herself to worry about. It was at that point in her thought processes that Sabrina relaxed completely.

"Would you like to meet Olivia?" Glynnis asked softly. "Michael's in school, but Livvy's back in the playroom."

"I'd love to." She'd heard the television in the back of the house. She braced herself as Glynnis left the room. Part of her was thrilled at the idea of having siblings; another part of her felt a darker emotion. She had always loved being her father's pet— "the child of my heart" —he'd always called her, and it had made Sabrina feel so special. But now...

And then Glynnis returned, holding the hand of a darling little girl. Sabrina's heart caught as she studied Olivia. *My sister.* Sabrina had always wanted a sister, and now she had one.

Olivia was beautiful, she thought, remarkably like her mother, with the same curly reddish-blond hair and hazel eyes. She grinned at Sabrina, causing two dimples—one in each cheek—to pop out.

"This is Olivia," Glynnis said, a proud smile on her face.

"Livvy," Olivia said.

"Hello, Livvy. It's very nice to meet you."

Olivia looked up at her mother, a frown replacing her smile. "She's big, Mommy." This was said as an accusation.

Gregg chuckled. In an aside to Sabrina, he said, "Glynnis told her she was going to meet her sister. She probably was envisioning a playmate."

Sabrina nodded. She was fighting back tears. She loved Olivia already, and she knew she would love Michael, too. She wondered how her father could have borne being away from them so much, because she knew he had been. Even if he had spent a lot of the time he had pretended to be traveling with them instead, he was still gone a lot.

"I'd love to play with you, Olivia," she said, crouching down to the child's level. "Do you like to play dolls?"

Olivia nodded solemnly.

"Well, maybe later, we can play dolls together. Okay?"

"Okay."

Glynnis rolled her eyes. "You may be sorry you said that," she warned. "Livvy never forgets anything."

Sabrina still hadn't seen anything in Olivia that reminded her of her father, but that wasn't unusual. Sabrina took after her mother, too. The only characteristic she and her dad shared was dark hair.

She knew the same wouldn't be true of Michael, for she'd seen his school picture framed in the hallway, and he looked so much like her father's childhood photos, it was eerie. Now she couldn't wait for the boy to come home from school so she could see him in person.

"Have you had lunch yet?" Glynnis asked.

"Just coffee an hour ago," Sabrina admitted.

"Let's go back to the kitchen, then. I've got homemade vegetable soup and fresh corn bread."

"That sounds wonderful."

During lunch, Gregg watched the two women getting to know each other. It was clear they liked each other. He wasn't surprised. They were a lot alike. Not in the way they looked—Glynnis was tall and Sabrina was petite, and their coloring was entirely different—but they had all the important things in common. Both were strong and intelligent, beautiful and warm. Now that their first awkwardness was over, they were chatting away like old pals. In fact, he could easily imagine them as friends, and he found himself wishing Sabrina lived here, because she would be a comfort to Glynnis and another source of support.

He hated when it was time for him to take off for the restaurant. He would have liked to stay the entire day, but the situation between Joe and Billy had escalated to the point where Gregg was afraid to be gone too long for fear all hell would break loose and one or the other would walk out. He guessed if things continued like this, he might have to let Billy go, no matter how much he hated to, because like it or not, he couldn't afford to lose his chef. Damn Joe, he thought angrily. Why did he have to be such a hard nose?

Getting up, he said, "I've got to take off. Sabrina, I'll come back and get you whenever you want to leave."

"I was planning on you being here for dinner and the evening, too," Glynnis said. "Gregg can come and get you after he's through at the restaurant or if you want to leave earlier, I can take you back to your motel."

"Listen, I can just call a cab," Sabrina said.

"You're not calling a cab," Gregg said. "I'll come back for you. Say about ten?"

"You know," Glynnis said thoughtfully, "why don't you cancel your motel reservation and stay here tonight? I've got a guest room, and I would so love to have you. We all would."

Sabrina hesitated. The offer was tempting. She was already besotted with Olivia, and she felt totally comfortable with Glynnis, but she was betraying her mother enough by coming here. It might be a small thing, but she couldn't help feeling staying at Glynnis's overnight would be the ultimate betrayal.

"Thank you," she said, "but I really can't."

Glynnis nodded. "I understand."

Oddly enough, Sabrina thought she did.

In no time, it seemed, it was three-thirty and Michael's car pool had dropped him off.

He smiled shyly at Sabrina when his mother introduced them. Sabrina's heart contracted as he stuck out his hand to shake hers. He looked even more like her father than his picture had shown. His hair was exactly the same shade of dark brown, and he even had the same cowlick at the crown. And his eyes were so like her father's, it was almost as if her father were there.

Standing there, the last of the anger and hurt her father had caused melted away.

"Michael, honey, do you have homework?" Glynnis asked.

"Uh-huh."

"You can do it while I start supper, then."

While Michael did his homework at the kitchen table—which consisted of coloring a picture of a pumpkin and another of a turkey—Sabrina helped Olivia color her own picture.

Glynnis bustled around the kitchen, first assembling all the ingredients she needed, then slicing a couple of onions and placing them in a hot skillet. They sizzled as they hit the pan, and Glynnis immediately lowered the gas under them. She filled a big pot with water and put it on to heat, then began to slice mushrooms. She was humming as she worked.

"You look like you enjoy cooking," Sabrina commented.

Glynnis smiled. "I love it. This recipe is one of Ben's fav—" She stopped abruptly. "I'm sorry."

"No, it's okay. It sure smells good. What is it?"

"Spaghetti with carmelized onions and mushrooms. It came out of one of my *Cooking Light* magazines."

"I'm not much of a cook," Sabrina confessed. Neither was her mother, but of course, her mother had never had to be. Sabrina couldn't help comparing her mother's situation with Glynnis's. She wondered how much insurance her father had taken out for Glynnis and the children. She hoped it was a lot. "What did you do before the children were born?" she asked curiously.

"I taught art and art history at the college level."

"That explains all the wonderful paintings I've

been admiring.'' The house was filled with watercolors.

''Thanks. In fact, my interest in art and art history is how I met Ben.'' She stopped. Looked at Sabrina. ''Do you want to hear this?''

''Yes. Yes, I do.'' Sabrina would never have asked, but she was dying to know about their relationship.

''I was spending the summer in Italy. Had done so for several years in a row. Florence, mostly, because of the museums and fabulous art. I'd made friends with a young woman—Ursula—who was a local guide to the Uffizi, and she called me one day to say she had the flu and could I possibly take an American tour group through the museum that afternoon.'' Glynnis smiled, remembering. ''It was one of your father's groups.''

''And he was there that day.''

''Yes, he was there.'' Her smile softened. ''I liked him immediately. He was so nice and so attentive. He seemed so interested in everything I said. It was very flattering.''

Yes, Sabrina's father had the knack of listening. When you talked to him, he always made you feel as if every word was important. He never acted as if he couldn't wait to get away or, as so many others did, was more concerned with what he was going to say next than with what you were saying then.

Glynnis finished slicing her mushrooms and added spaghetti to the pot of water that had begun to boil.

"Anyway, when the tour of the museum was over, the group had free time, and they all left, but he hung around to talk to me and invited me to have coffee with him. He said I'd done a great job and was I interested in doing more local tours. I explained that I was just there for the summer and would be returning to my job at the college the end of August." She stirred the cooking spaghetti, then looked at Sabrina. "We talked for hours and ended by having dinner together that night. Ben extended his stay in Italy, and we saw each other every day until I had to leave."

Listening to Glynnis, it was almost as if Glynnis wasn't talking about herself and Sabrina's father but was instead telling a story about two other people—people Sabrina didn't know—so what was revealed couldn't possibly hurt her. She was dying to know if they'd been lovers by then, but of course, she couldn't ask.

"After I came home to Ivy, we were in constant touch by phone and e-mail, and as often as he could, Ben would come here to see me. I knew I was in love with him, and I thought he loved me, too, but he never mentioned the future, and after about a year of this, I brought it up." Her expression was apologetic. "Did you know that? That it was me who pushed getting married?"

"Yes."

Glynnis sighed. "Oh, good. I wasn't sure if you knew."

"My father wrote that in the letter he left me. But he said he didn't blame you. He said the thing was, he couldn't give you up, that's why he didn't tell you the truth." Sabrina didn't feel disloyal to her mother by telling Glynnis this much. After all, none of what she'd said was a criticism of her mother. And to Glynnis's credit, she hadn't asked about Sabrina's mother, although Sabrina was sure she was very curious.

"Anyway, we got married shortly after that, and you know the rest," Glynnis finished.

"Are you sorry? Now that you know the truth?"

Glynnis shook her head. "No. How could I be? Marrying Ben gave me Michael and Olivia."

Sabrina looked at the children. Olivia was biting her bottom lip, so intent was she on her coloring, and Michael, who had finished his two pictures, was helping his sister with hers. Their sweet innocence pierced Sabrina's heart. No, in Glynnis's shoes, Sabrina wouldn't be sorry, either. These children were truly a gift from God.

Sabrina wondered if she would ever have children. So far she hadn't met anyone with whom she would want to. On the heels of that thought, the image of Gregg's face flashed through her mind.

Stop that, she told herself sternly. She couldn't even imagine what her mother would have to say if Sabrina were to be foolhardy enough to try to make Gregg a part of her life.

Gregg Antonelli is off-limits.

Period.

Chapter Five

After helping in the kitchen for a couple of hours, Gregg finally headed into his office about four o'clock. With luck, he could get in an hour or two of work on the books before the dinner rush.

He groaned as he eyed the stack of bills and mail on his desk. No way he was going to get all that taken care of in a couple of hours. Maybe he'd better bite the bullet and hire someone to at least do the payroll, receivables and payables. As he scribbled himself a reminder to call a couple of bookkeeping services he'd seen advertised, his phone buzzed.

"What now?" he muttered.

"Gregg? Your cousin Steve is on line two."

Gregg's irritation gave way to a pleased smile.

"Steve! Hey, cuz. How's it going? It's been a long time." Steve was the son of Gregg's Uncle Anthony, his father's younger brother. Steve had always been a favorite of Gregg's, even though there was fifteen years difference in their ages. The kid had graduated from college in May and taken a job with a medical supply company in San Francisco. Gregg had only talked to him once since. He'd been meaning to call the younger man for weeks.

"Hey, yourself," Steve said. "Things are great with me. What about you?"

"Well, things here are in kind of a mess right now."

"What's wrong? Trouble with the restaurant?"

"Nothing out of the ordinary. No, it's Glynnis."

"Yeah, Dad told me about her husband dying. I sent her a card."

"She told me. But your dad doesn't know the whole story." Gregg quickly filled Steve in.

Steve whistled when he'd finished. "Man, that sucks."

"Yeah, it does. I wish I had more time to spend with her, but it's tough to get away from here for more than a few hours at a time."

"Maybe I can help."

"You? What can you do? You're in San Francisco."

"No more."

"What do you mean, no more?"

"Just that. I quit that job, and I'm back home."

"In Chicago?"

"Yeah. And I was thinking…"

Gregg chuckled. "Oh, oh, that's dangerous."

"I'm serious."

"Sorry. So you were thinking what?"

"I was thinking I'd like to come and work for you."

"What?"

"I've been thinking about this for a while."

"To do what? Wait tables?"

"That and anything else you need help with. I want to learn the business."

Gregg was floored. Sure, Steve had always shown an interest in the restaurant. In fact, the summer before it had opened, Steve had come to Ivy and helped Gregg get the premises ready. They'd painted and sanded and refinished and replaced, and he'd worked every bit as hard as Gregg had and seemed to enjoy every minute. So had Gregg.

"What about your degree? I thought you were thinking about applying to medical school."

"That's what the folks want me to do. And I did think about it. But medicine is not for me."

Now that Gregg was over his first surprise, he realized it would be a godsend to have Steve here. The kid was smart, and he was a hard worker. He would be a real help to Gregg, and once he learned the business, he'd be invaluable, because he was family. "Have you talked to your parents about this? I mean,

I'd love to have you, but I don't want them getting mad at me.''

''I've talked to them. They're cool with it.''

''I can't pay you a lot to start.''

''I know that. But if I'm bunking in with you, I won't need a whole lot. Unless you don't want me staying with you? You haven't got a girlfriend I don't know about, do you?''

''No, no girlfriend.'' An image of Sabrina flashed through his mind. He shook it away. ''When could you come?''

''I can be there this weekend.''

After they hung up, Gregg smiled. Things were looking up. They were definitely looking up.

Sabrina was sorry to see the day end. She couldn't remember when she'd enjoyed being with someone as much as she'd enjoyed being with Glynnis and the children.

If only she could be a part of…

No.

She couldn't even allow the thought to be completed. All the ''if onlys'' in the world wouldn't change reality. The fact was, Glynnis and the children could never be a part of Sabrina's life.

It had been wonderful to meet them, good for her to see what it was that had caused her father to do what he had done, but this meeting had to be the end of their association.

Because as much as she might like to, Sabrina

could not continue seeing Glynnis. Sabrina's mother had been hurt enough, and the last thing Sabrina wanted to do was cause additional trauma.

So it was with a mixture of sadness and regret that she said goodbye. While Gregg looked on, the two women hugged.

"I wish you were staying longer," Glynnis said.

"I do, too."

Sabrina could see that Glynnis dared not say everything else she was thinking, just as Sabrina couldn't. Her heart was heavy as she knelt down to hug and kiss Michael and Olivia.

"Bye," Michael said shyly. Then he shoved the picture of the turkey he'd been coloring into her hand. "This is for you."

Deeply touched by the gesture, Sabrina said, "Oh, Michael. How nice of you to give this to me. But isn't it your homework?"

"Uh-huh, but we don't have to bring it back. Miss Gleason said we could give it to our mother."

"But I'm not your mother," Sabrina said, glancing up at Glynnis, who smiled.

"I know," Michael said seriously. "You're my sister!" This last was said with a triumphant grin.

"I'll treasure this always." Sabrina knew she would never forget the sweet smile on his face, and the way he looked at her so trustingly. She had a lump the size of Alaska in her throat. Why was life so unfair sometimes?

Next Olivia put her chubby arms around Sabrina's

neck and gave her a kiss. Sabrina blinked back tears as she hugged the little girl to her.

Gregg obviously sensed her fragile emotions and didn't try to engage her in conversation as he drove her back to her motel. Sabrina was grateful. The wrong word might have sent her over the edge. Too much had happened in too short a space of time. Her brain and heart were on sensory overload.

When they reached the motel, he waited while she checked in, then he drove her around the back and parked in front of her door.

"What time are you planning to leave in the morning?" he asked as she unlocked the door.

"About eight. Will there be much traffic then?"

"There shouldn't be. Are you planning to have breakfast first?"

"Probably."

"How about if I come and get you around seven? There's a restaurant a couple of blocks from here that has a terrific breakfast buffet."

"You don't have to do that."

"I know I don't have to. I want to."

"Thank you." She tried to smile but knew it was a feeble attempt. Once more, she was near tears. Ducking her head, she fought to gain control of herself.

"Hey, are you gonna be okay?"

She nodded, reluctantly meeting his gaze. "Yes. I—I'm just…you know…"

He grimaced. "I know. It's been an emotional day. For Glynnis, too."

"Yes." *Dammit. She was going to cry.*

"She really liked you."

"I liked her, too." She knuckled away the tears, furious with herself.

"Listen, I know it's tough, but I think things will work out. It'll just take some time, that's all."

Sabrina nodded. She wasn't so sure. How could they work out? Nothing would change the facts.

After Gregg left, she kept thinking about what he'd said as she prepared for bed. She knew he had been trying to make her feel better, but it hadn't worked. Time wouldn't make any difference. Glynnis and the children would always be off-limits to her, at least for as long as her mother was alive.

And Sabrina certainly didn't want anything to happen to her mother. What she wanted was what her Granny Rockwell used to say was having her cake and eating it, too. The impossible, in other words.

She was in the middle of brushing her teeth and was still thinking about Gregg and Glynnis and the children and everything that had happened that day when her cell phone rang. It startled her, and her heart was beating too fast when she answered.

"Sabrina?" It was her mother.

Guilt immediately flooded Sabrina, almost as if her mother had somehow divined her thoughts. "Mom? Is something wrong?"

"No. I just thought I'd call and see how your day went."

"Oh." For a moment, Sabrina couldn't remember where she was supposed to be and what she was supposed to be doing. That's what happened when you told lies. "It...it was fine."

"You don't seem sure."

"No, I—I was just thinking about something else, and had to get my brain in gear, that's all."

"You got your interview okay?"

"Yes, everything went like clockwork." Sabrina's guilty feelings intensified. She hated inventing stories about fictitious interviews to tell to her mother. "How about you? Did you have a good day?"

"How could I?" her mother said, the bitterness and anger that had been so prevalent lately creeping back into her voice. "Everywhere I go, people stare. They're *gloating* over our downfall, Sabrina. Simply gloating."

"I'm sure some people are, but our real friends aren't."

"I don't have any real friends."

"Oh, Mom, that's not true. Leland is a wonderful friend. So is Florence. And what about Virginia and Katherine and Libby?" Sabrina had named her mother's longtime bridge buddies.

"Those three are the worst."

Sabrina sighed. "I think you're exaggerating. If anything, I'm sure they feel badly for you."

"That's because you don't really know them. Besides, I don't want their pity!"

"Mom…"

"You don't understand. It's not the same for you as it is for me. Don't you see, Sabrina? Your father might as well have hung a sign around my neck saying Cast Off For a New Model."

"But you weren't cast off. He didn't leave you."

"Don't you *dare* defend him! Anyone who could do what he did doesn't deserve any sympathy. *I'm* the one who deserves your sympathy."

Sabrina couldn't help but remember how compassionate and concerned Glynnis had been when Sabrina talked briefly about her mother, how Glynnis was able to put herself in another's place, whereas Sabrina's mother could only think of her own misery.

"I'll never forgive your father," Isabel continued. "Never."

"It would be better for you if you could," Sabrina said before she could stop herself.

"Don't you start preaching to me, Sabrina. You have no *idea* what it's like to be in my shoes."

"I'm sorry, Mother. I know I don't. It's just that I'm tired. It's been a long day. A long couple of weeks. We should both get some sleep."

"Yes, well…you're coming home tomorrow, aren't you? I told Bob Culberson you were."

"Bob Culberson?"

"Yes, he called earlier today and wanted to talk to you. He said there were some decisions that needed to be made, and he wanted to discuss them with us.''

Oh, God. This was *all* she needed. One more thing dumped on her. Sabrina sighed. ''When I get home, I'll call him.''

''What time will you be back tomorrow?''

''I should be in the office by noon.''

''Call me when you get there. I worry about you on the road.''

''I'll be careful. And yes, I'll call you when I get to the paper.''

After the phone call, Sabrina continued getting ready for bed, but the conversation with her mother had unsettled her, and she knew it would be useless to try to go to sleep. She wished she had something to read. She'd forgotten to stuff a book in her overnight bag.

Picking up the television guide provided by the motel, she looked at the offerings. Nothing interested her. She looked at the clock. Eleven-fifteen. She eyed the phone again. Casey would still be up. A night owl, she rarely went to bed before midnight. Needing to talk to someone she didn't have to pretend with, Sabrina picked up her cell phone and punched in Casey's number.

''Sabrina! What's up? Where are you? I called the paper today and they said you'd gone out of town.''

''I'm in Ivy.''

''So you decided to go, huh? Well? How was it? Or haven't you met her yet?''

"I met both her and the children. I spent the day with them."

"Tell me everything!"

Sabrina smiled. She could just see Casey getting comfortable, probably sitting Indian fashion on her futon and leaning forward eagerly. Sabrina felt better already. Talking to Casey always made her feel better.

"Well?" Casey said. "I'm waiting."

So Sabrina started at the beginning and told her everything.

"Oh, man," Casey said when she was done. "You're in trouble."

"What do you mean?"

"You know what I mean. You like her. And you love the kids. Plus you're attracted to the sexy brother. The way I see it, there's no way you're not going to see these people again."

"Casey! I can't see them again. It's impossible. And I'm *not* attracted to the sexy brother," she added as an afterthought.

"*Is* it impossible? And you *are* attracted to him. Don't lie to me, Sabrina. I know you too well."

"You know it's impossible. Okay, I think he's attractive, yes, but I'm not *attracted* to him."

Casey chuckled. "Uh-huh. Tell me another one."

"Well, I'm not."

"Fine. Lie to yourself if you want to. For right now, let's forget the brother and talk about Glynnis and the kids. Hell, Sabrina, you *should* be a part of their life. Those kids are your half sister and brother. I think it'd be a crime *not* to get to know them.''

"But how? You know my mother. She'd go ballistic if she found out.''

"Why don't you just tell your mother the truth? She's not made of glass. She won't break.''

"You make it sound so easy.''

"It *is* easy. Just say, Mother, I've met Dad's other family and I intend to continue seeing them. Yeah, she'll go ballistic, but she'll get over it.''

"Do you really think so?''

"Yeah, I do.''

"Casey…''

"Well…maybe not. But she's not gonna cut you out of her life. How can she? You're all she's got.''

Unsaid was what they both knew Casey thought: that Isabel March could have had a fuller, richer life if she'd been a different kind of person. That it was her own fault Sabrina was all she had. And that Sabrina had suffered for it long enough.

"So I say go for it,'' Casey continued. "And the sooner, the better.''

Sabrina sighed.

"You never told me what she said about the kids. She *does* know about them now, doesn't she?''

"Yes. Leland told her.''

"Were you there when he did?''

"No. He said he thought it would be easier on her if I wasn't.'' That he was willing to do so still puzzled Sabrina, even though she'd been so glad to escape having to see the pain the knowledge would bring her mother, she'd been cowardly and taken him up on his generous offer.

"Has she talked to you about them since?"

"No. It's like she doesn't know."

"And you haven't pushed it."

"No. We're both pretending the children don't exist. I guess it's easier for her that way. Maybe she's hoping no one else will ever find out about them."

"She could be right. I mean, if Leland says nothing and you say nothing...your father didn't leave them anything in his will, did he?"

"No. There was no mention of either Glynnis or the children in his will."

"Are they gonna get anything?"

"He had an insurance policy in Glynnis's name."

"Well, she could be right, then."

They both fell silent. Then Casey said, "So tell me about this brother that you find attractive and sexy but aren't the least bit interested in." There was teasing laughter in her voice.

"I really don't know much to tell. The two times I've been in his company, we've either talked about what my dad did or we've talked about his sister and the kids."

"Well, is he sending any vibes?"

Sabrina thought about the way Gregg looked at her. "Kind of. I think."

"You *think?* Girl, when a guy is sending vibes, you know it. So is he or isn't he?"

"I guess he is, but he knows as well as I do that it's a go-nowhere kind of thing, so it doesn't mean anything."

"If you told your mother the truth, it *could* go somewhere."

"Casey, I'll concede that it might, in the far distant future, be possible for me to have some kind of relationship with Glynnis and the children, but it will *never* be possible to have a relationship with her brother. So can we please talk about something else now?"

When Gregg walked into his apartment after dropping Sabrina off, the first thing he spied was the blinking light on his answering machine.

He pressed the play button. "Gregg? It's Glynnis. Call me when you get home. I'll be up."

Frowning, he quickly punched in her number. "Glynnis?" he said when she answered. "Is something wrong?"

"No, no, I just... I wanted to talk to you."

Sinking down into his favorite lounge chair, he kicked off his loafers and settled back. "Okay, I'm listening."

"You got her back to the motel okay?"

"Yeah. But that's not why you called."

"No. I—I just wanted to say how much I liked her."

"She liked you, too."

"Oh, Gregg, this is such a mess, isn't it?"

"What is it, Glynnie? You seem more upset now than you have been since the day I told you about Ben."

She was silent for a few seconds. "I don't know. Somehow meeting Sabrina, it just brought home to me how complicated everything is. The thing is, I want her to be a part of our lives. I want the children to know her. I want us to be friends. And I'm afraid that's an impossible wish. I'm afraid we won't see her again, and that makes me sad."

Gregg wished he had some magic words for her, but all he could think of to say was what he'd told Sabrina, that somehow things would work out.

"Do you really think so?"

He heard the hopeful note in her voice. Torn between being honest and making her feel better, he decided on honesty. "I don't know. I hope so. Maybe, with time."

"Gregg, you don't have to answer this if you don't want to, but—"

"What?"

"Has Sabrina said anything to you about her mother?"

"Not a lot." He hesitated, then decided Glynnis deserved to know as much of the truth as possible. "I do know her mother is in a wheelchair."

"Oh, my God. What...what's wrong with her?"

"She had a skiing accident that left her paralyzed from the waist down."

"No wonder Ben couldn't leave her."

He wanted to tell her to quit making excuses for Ben, but once again he told himself there was no point.

"Do you think—?" She abruptly stopped.

"Think what?" When she didn't answer, he said it again. "Think what, Glynnie?"

She sighed deeply. "I just wondered. Maybe I could call her."

He frowned. "Call who? Sabrina?"

"No. Not Sabrina. Her mother."

"What?"

"Well, maybe she'd like to talk—"

"Don't even *think* about it, Glynnis."

"But Gregg, you don't know her. Maybe she'd like to talk to me. Maybe it would bring her some comfort or something. I just feel I should do something to try to make things better."

"It's not a good idea."

"But—"

"Here's why it's not. Sabrina said her mother was very bitter and very angry."

"Oh."

"I hope you and Sabrina will be able to build some kind of relationship in the future. But if you were thinking it might eventually include her mother, that all of you might end up one big, happy family…that's a fantasy."

Later, in that twilight zone between wakefulness and sleep, Gregg realized that he, too, had been entertaining a fantasy, one where he and Sabrina might also have a relationship. He wondered what Glynnis would say if she knew. She'd probably tell him his fantasy was no more attainable than hers.

Chapter Six

Sabrina was ready and waiting when Gregg pulled his Explorer into the parking lot. Grabbing her overnight bag, she took one last look around the room to make sure she hadn't forgotten anything, then let herself out the door.

"Good morning."

"Good morning." Today he wore a brown leather bomber jacket and aviator sunglasses. She thought about how she'd told Casey he was attractive. Gregg Antonelli was more than attractive. He was gorgeous. Why, oh why did he have to be Glynnis's brother?

He reached for her overnight bag.

"I'm just going to follow you to the restaurant," she said. "That way, when we're finished, I can hit the road."

"Okay." He smiled. "You look nice this morning."

Her heart skipped under his smile. Those dimples were enough to make any woman melt, Sabrina thought helplessly. "Thanks." She unlocked her car.

As he opened the driver's side door for her, Sabrina caught a whiff of his cologne or maybe it was his aftershave. Whatever it was, it was woodsy and masculine and sexy and it suddenly made her want to fling her arms around him and tell him to carry her off somewhere. She couldn't help it, she laughed.

"What's so funny?"

"Oh, nothing. I'm just being silly this morning." She knew she was blushing and hoped he couldn't tell.

"I've embarrassed you."

Oh, shoot. He *could* tell. *Settle down, Sabrina, before you make a total fool of yourself.* "I embarrass easily."

He grinned. "I don't know about you, but I'm starving."

"I'm dying for coffee, personally."

"Well, let's go, then."

Once they were in the restaurant, seated across from each other in a booth, Sabrina felt a bit more in control of herself. Having the table between them helped.

"Do you want to look at the menu? Or do you want to try the buffet?" he asked.

"What are you going to do?"

"I love the buffet. The biscuits and cream gravy are enough to make a sane man go crazy."

She laughed. "You've talked me into it."

Once they'd filled their plates and were again seated, he said, "Did you sleep okay last night?" He shook out his napkin.

Sabrina shrugged. "Yeah. Took me awhile to get to sleep, though. My mother called and after we talked, I couldn't settle down."

His blue eyes studied her. "Does your mother know where you are?"

"No. Whenever I go anywhere I tell her to call me on my cell phone." She sighed. "She thinks I'm in Columbus on a story."

"Do you plan to tell her about coming to Ivy?"

Sabrina shook her head. "I wish I could, but I'm afraid she'd come unglued."

"Listen, if I'm out of line, tell me, but I'd like to know more about your mother."

"What do you want to know?"

"For starters, what kind of injury does she have?"

"She damaged her spinal cord."

"Boy, that's rough."

"Yes."

"Do you think that's why your father—?"

"No. Their…their marriage was in trouble before the accident. In fact—" She stopped. She shouldn't be telling him this. And yet, why not? Who would it hurt now? Her father was dead. And her mother was never going to meet Gregg or Glynnis. They certainly weren't going to spread gossip about her. "My father had asked my mother for a divorce. She got very angry and left for the ski trip the next day. While there, she had her accident. After that, Dad was very devoted. But I know he was lonely. My…my mother is not a warm woman. And I think she blamed him for the accident."

"Was it his fault?"

"No, he wasn't even there. But she blamed him, anyway." In a burst of honesty, she added, "My mother always blames other people for her problems."

He didn't seem to know what to say to that. Sabrina picked up her fork and began to eat. After a moment, he did, too. She couldn't imagine what had possessed her to say such a thing, especially to someone who was almost a stranger. And yet, Gregg seemed to have that effect on her. She found herself wanting to tell him all kinds of things. And she wanted, in return, to know all kinds of things about him.

"What about your parents?" she said after a while. "When did they die?"

Gregg cut a piece of sausage. "They died in a car accident when Glynnis and I were sixteen. They were both in their early forties."

"How terrible." Sabrina couldn't help thinking of her father, who had also died young.

"Yes. It was hard on Glynnis, especially. She and Dad were especially close."

"But at least you have each other. And now you've got Michael and Olivia, too." Sabrina tried not to feel envious, but it was hard. He had someone with whom to share the tough times, and she had no one.

She ate the last bit of biscuit and gravy on her plate. "How'd you get into the restaurant business?"

"I worked as a waiter the summer before college, then part-time for the next couple of years. When I found myself looking forward to the hours at the restaurant more than the hours in school, I knew somebody was trying to tell me something." He grinned. "I've been working in the business ever since."

"How long have you owned Antonelli's?"

"Six years."

"Did you buy it from someone?"

"No. I bought the building, which had housed another restaurant for a while, but it had gone out of business a couple of years before I entered the picture. And it wasn't an Italian restaurant. Antonelli's is strictly my creation."

Sabrina wondered where he'd gotten the money to start the restaurant. Although she didn't know much about the business, she knew enough to know that it cost a lot to launch any new business. In addition to the building itself, there was equipment, supplies, salaries, advertising and promotion and who knows what else. Of course, if there was another restaurant there before, the kitchen would have already been furnished, but still...

"The building was in bad shape when I bought it. It needed a lot of work, both inside and out. I had some of it done, and my cousin Steve and I did the rest ourselves."

"Do you still love the business?" she asked. Motioning to their waitress, she pointed to her coffee cup, which needed a refill.

"Yes. It's in my blood." He waited until the waitress had given them refills on their coffee. "What about you? Do you like your job?"

"I used to."

He gave her a quizzical look.

She sighed. "It's a long story." She went on to tell him about the paper, how it was a family business and how she'd practically grown up there. "I was a paper carrier as a kid, and then, when my uncle took over, he used to let me work back in the production department. That was before computers—when we did all the pasteup by hand."

"Did you study journalism in college?"

"Yes. I never wanted to do anything else. But for the past couple of years, when the majority of my time has had to be given to the management of the paper, things have been different."

He studied her thoughtfully. "And you feel trapped."

She stared at him. "Yes."

"It's a big responsibility, carrying on a family legacy. What would happen if you left? Would the paper fold?"

"No. There are lots of capable people we could hire to run it. In fact, there's a man working for me now who could take over."

"But..."

"But." She closed her eyes for a moment. How to make him understand. "But a Rockwell has always been at the helm. It would kill my mother if I quit. Especially now when she feels so betrayed by my father."

"Sabrina, look, I know this isn't any of my business, but I don't think your leaving would kill your mother."

"Not literally, of course. But..." She sighed again and looked away. "She's had so many disappointments."

"If you *could* leave, what would you like to do?"

She smiled. "That's easy. I'd like to freelance. Write articles. Maybe even do a column for newspapers and try to sell it."

"What kind of column?"

Sabrina hesitated. She had never told anyone about her idea. She'd always been afraid that if she talked about it, she'd somehow jinx it. But now, with Gregg, she wanted to talk about it. "Well, you know how there are so many columns in syndication that address women's issues?"

"Yeah." He grinned. "I don't read them, but I know they're there."

"There's nothing for the young, single woman except dating, fashion and makeup, that kind of thing.

Everything serious is geared toward older women. I'd like to write about issues that twenty-somethings and early thirty-somethings face. Jobs and living on your own for the first time and learning how to handle money and dealing with parents who don't want to let you grow up and how to make the right choices. Even politics and world affairs. There are unlimited subjects. It's a niche that's crying to be filled.''

He was smiling when she stopped talking. ''Anything that excites you this much is something you should do.''

She toyed with her coffee cup. ''Before my father died, we talked about my leaving the paper. He encouraged me to. And I was seriously considering it.''

''And then he died.''

''Yes.''

Yes, Sabrina thought. And then he died. And her world had gone up in smoke. Sadness gripped her. Fighting it, she looked at her watch. It was almost eight. ''Oh, gosh, it's late. I should be going.''

He motioned to the waitress. After paying the bill, they walked out to her car.

''Thanks for everything, Gregg. You made this visit a lot easier for me than I thought it would be.''

''It meant a lot to Glynnis that you came.''

''It meant a lot to me, too. I only wish…well, you know what I wish, and it's impossible.'' She looked away.

''Sabrina.'' He touched her cheek, turning her to

face him again. The sadness in her eyes tugged at his heart. He was suddenly filled with a fierce desire to take care of this woman, an emotion that was disquieting, because he'd never felt this way about anyone other than his sister. Impulsively he put his arms around her. "I know you can't come here again. But would it be all right if I came to Rockwell to see you?"

Sabrina wasn't sure she'd heard him correctly. Then her heart leaped as his words sank in. He wanted to see her again! Happiness flooded her. All the reasons why seeing him again wouldn't be a good idea flew out of her mind.

Despite this euphoria, there was still a small part of her that knew she should say no, yet she couldn't make her lips form the word.

"I know this is nuts," he continued urgently. "I've never believed that crap about love at first sight, but from the moment I met you, something in me knew you were the woman I've been waiting for all of my life."

The words pummeled Sabrina, and her heart beat crazily. They stared into each other's eyes for a long moment, then he dipped his head and kissed her deeply and hungrily, as if he could never get enough of her. She clung to him, returning his kisses with all the pent-up longing she'd been pretending wasn't there.

When they finally broke apart, they were both breathing hard. Sabrina was so stunned she couldn't have spoken if her life depended on it, and she could see he was equally shaken.

A car pulled into the slot next to hers, and Sabrina reluctantly pulled away.

"Gregg, I—"

"Shh," he said, putting his finger over her mouth. "Don't say anything. It's okay. I know you have to go. I'll call you tonight, all right? We'll talk then."

Silently she nodded. Her head was spinning.

He waited while she got into her car. As she pulled out of the parking lot, she looked in her rearview mirror. He was still standing there watching her.

Gregg drove to the restaurant in a daze.

He couldn't believe what had just happened. What had come over him? He hadn't lost control like that since he was a horny teenager at St. Ambrose High School and lusting after Mary Theresa Flynn.

He thought about what he'd said to Sabrina. The words had seemed to come from nowhere. He certainly hadn't *planned* to say them. But even now, away from her physical influence, he knew they were true.

That he could feel this way about a woman after only seeing her twice told the entire story.

He was in love.

He wondered what his buddies would say when they found out. After his broken engagement, he knew they all thought he would never get caught again. That's how they referred to falling in love:

getting caught. He smiled. Hell, who cared what they thought? He had fallen in love—for real this time—and right now, that's all that mattered.

So no matter what the odds against him and Sabrina—and there were a lot—a *helluva* lot!—the bottom line was, he wanted her, and he'd do whatever it took to get her.

For hours afterward, Sabrina could still feel the imprint of Gregg's lips on her own. If she hadn't, she might have thought she'd imagined the whole episode, because she had never expected anything like what had happened between them in the restaurant parking lot.

From the moment I met you, something in me knew you were the woman I've been waiting for all of my life…

Over and over she replayed what Gregg had said. And no matter how many times she relived that moment of hearing the words for the first time, the thrill was never any less.

Gregg…

Her mind kept whispering his name.

Gregg.

Was there ever such a wonderful name? Such a wonderful man? Such a wonderful feeling? She couldn't remember feeling so giddy and so heedless of the consequences of where she might be heading.

For most of her life Sabrina had been responsible and practical. She had rarely, if ever, given in to impulsive actions. Probably because of her mother's influence, Sabrina had always been conscious of her place in the universe.

If Isabel had said it once, she'd said it a thousand times. *You are a Rockwell, and don't ever forget it. You have a certain image to uphold and that means you have to be better than everyone else. You can't afford to do stupid things. Think, Sabrina, think hard before you act. Always consider how your actions will look to everyone else.*

Sabrina sighed as the weight of those words bore down upon her. She was so tired of being a Rockwell. So tired of caring what others thought. So tired of her circumspect, unexciting life.

I deserve to be happy, don't I?

But even as she asked the question, she wondered if she would be able to live with the price of that happiness.

"Sabrina. Sabrina?"

Sabrina jumped at the sound of her name. Jan Kellogg, her advertising manager, stood in front of her desk. "I'm sorry, Jan, did you say something?"

Jan's green eyes sparkled with amusement. "Well, *yeah.* For at least the last ten seconds."

"I must have been daydreaming." That wasn't exactly the right word. Mooning was more like it.

Jan flicked an imaginary speck of lint off her black slacks. "I just wondered if you'd looked over those proposed rate sheets I worked up. I'd like to start giving them out to customers so they are prepared for the upcoming hike.''

Sabrina nodded. ''Yes, I did The only problem I've got is with the monthly discount. We've been giving twenty percent for eight years now. I'm not sure we can afford to decrease it to ten.''

Jan frowned and sat on the chair next to Sabrina's desk. ''I know. I'm a little concerned about that myself, but Sabrina, I've done my research. Ten percent is what the *Marienville Monitor* gives, and let's face it—where else will the advertisers go? We're the only game in town.''

''There's direct mail.''

''People in Rockwell don't respond to direct mail the way they respond to ads in the paper. That's why our advertisers stick with us. Believe me, it's not because they're loyal. If they got better value out of coupons or anything else, they'd be outta here like a shot.''

Sabrina bit her lip. Jan was right, but Sabrina couldn't help it. She hated raising advertising rates, even when she knew it was necessary and justified. She knew what a blow it had been to her when the price of newsprint had skyrocketed, but the inescapable fact was the paper could not continue doing business without a rate hike. The increase in the cost of health insurance alone had nearly wiped out all the profit from the additional advertising Jan had brought in during her first six months with the paper.

"They'll probably cut the size of their ads," she finally said.

"If they do, that only means the paper will be smaller and cost less to produce. We'll still come out ahead."

"How about if we compromise? Do what that paper in North Carolina does—the one I told you about. Give twenty percent off for a year's contract."

Jan considered the suggestion. "We could. Yeah, I like that. Shoot, if advertisers will commit for a year, that'll give us more time to work on bringing in new business."

Sabrina smiled wearily. Well, at least that problem was solved. For now at least. She handed the proposed rate sheet back to Jan. "Go ahead and add that additional yearly discount, then have it printed up."

"You don't want to see it first?"

Sabrina shook her head. "Nope. I trust you."

"Great." Jan turned to walk away, then stopped and turned around again. Her smile was teasing. "Before I go, I'm just curious. Who's the guy?"

"What guy?"

"The guy who's got you so besotted."

Sabrina could feel herself blushing. "It's that obvious, huh?"

Jan laughed. "Yeah, I know the signs. Who is it? Anyone I know? Anyone I wish I'd met first?"

Sabrina grinned. But she remained silent. She wasn't ready to tell anyone about Gregg, even if she didn't reveal his name. Her feelings for him were too new. She wanted to savor that newness and keep it to herself awhile longer. Of course, Casey knew about him, but she was the only one.

After Jan walked away, Sabrina tried to empty her mind of everything but work, but it got harder as the day wore on. She was going to see Gregg tomorrow night. He was returning from a three-day conference in New York and flying directly in to the Akron airport, and she was picking him up there. She'd made a reservation for him at the Just Like Home Motel, which was located on the highway about two miles outside of Rockwell. He had gotten an old friend to cover for him at the restaurant and planned to spend the entire weekend with her.

Only a week had passed since they'd said goodbye in Ivy. In some ways, the week had flown. In others, it had dragged interminably, filled with problems Sabrina didn't want to face. The meeting with Bob Culberson at her father's office was one of them. Bob had told them an offer had come in from one of the large tour companies to buy out March Tours.

"It's a good offer," he said. "I think you should take it."

"Sell the company?" Sabrina's mother said. "But why? You've been running it. Can't you keep running it?"

"Yes, I've been taking care of the day-to-day operation, but Ben was the one who went out and negotiated all the deals, Isabel. I can't do everything.

You're going to have to do something soon, anyway, because I promised Elaine I'd retire next year.''

''Sabrina and I will talk about this and let you know,'' Isabel said.

All the way home, Isabel had complained. ''You'd think he'd be a bit more loyal, wouldn't you?''

''Mom. He has a right to quit working if he wants to.''

''Must you *always* argue with me? Just once I wish you'd see *my* side of things.''

Sabrina didn't answer. What was the use? She and her mother never saw eye-to-eye on anything. If Sabrina had still been staying at her mother's, she wouldn't have been able to stand it.

She owed her peace of mind to her Aunt Irene, who had extended her stay in Rockwell for the second time and would be there until the coming weekend.

Sabrina's mother had made noises about Sabrina moving back to the house. ''Just until I feel better,'' she'd said plaintively.

Sabrina felt horrible refusing. ''I'm sorry, Mom, but I just can't. It's not like you're alone. Florence is here every day.''

''She's not family.''

''That never bothered you before.''

''Things are different now.''

It was difficult not to cave in to her mother's implied criticism, because Sabrina felt so guilty as it was, but she knew she couldn't. If she gave in and moved back home, even temporarily, she would never be free to have any kind of life of her own.

Sabrina was so excited she got to the Akron-Canton airport almost an hour early. At least she'd had the presence of mind to bring a book along. It was one she'd been wanting to read for ages, so she found a seat in the waiting area—one where she could watch the gate—and opened the book.

Thirty minutes later, she'd read only two pages, and she couldn't have told you what those pages were about. She put the book back into her tote. She was too on edge to read.

Instead, she people-watched, one of her favorite things to do. Often she made up stories about the people she saw, giving them whole histories. She settled her gaze on a harried-looking young mother, who was scolding a little boy who looked to be about two. He was adorable, Sabrina thought and wondered what he could have done to upset his mother so badly. As she watched, the mother suddenly stopped reproving him and gathered him up for a hug.

"I wuv you, Mommy," he said, patting her face.

Sabrina smiled and contentedly watched them until it was time to get up and check on Gregg's flight. She found the flight on the arrivals monitor. On Time, it said. She headed over to the place where arriving passengers would exit if they didn't have to go to baggage claim, which Gregg had said he wouldn't.

She didn't have long to wait. About ten minutes later, she saw him striding toward her, a huge grin on his face. Her heart somersaulted.

The moment he reached her side, he dropped his bag and enfolded her into his arms. His kiss made her dizzy, and she was laughing shakily when he released her.

Picking up his bag with his left hand, he put his right arm firmly around her shoulders. "God, it's good to see you."

"You, too." She knew she was grinning like a fool.

He kept his arm around her all the way out to the parking area. When they reached her car, he dropped the bag again and drew her close.

"I couldn't concentrate on work or the conference or anything this week for thinking about you," he muttered.

Sabrina's heart skidded as he leaned down, capturing her mouth once more. When his tongue delved, she was lost. She wrapped her arms around his neck and gave herself up to his kisses.

There was no telling how long they would have stood there kissing, but reality returned when a car filled with kids passed them, and the kids whistled. Pulling away from Gregg, Sabrina blushed.

Gregg laughed softly. "I can't wait until we're alone." His voice was husky, his eyes caressing as they swept over her face.

Sabrina could hardly breathe. She could see in his

eyes and hear in his voice what it was he wanted. He wanted to make love to her. He *intended* to make love to her, probably just as soon as they got to the motel. Her heart hammered. Was this what she wanted?

You know it's what you want. Why else did you wear the sexiest, prettiest underwear you own?

Birth control wasn't an issue, because she'd been on the pill for more than a year now—not because she'd been in a relationship but because she'd had some problems with her menstrual period, and her gynecologist had recommended the pill. For the first time since it had been prescribed, Sabrina was thankful, because now, no matter what happened or didn't happen, she was prepared.

During the drive from Akron to Rockwell, making love with Gregg was all she could think about. It seemed so reckless. She had only known this man a few weeks. Only been in his company a few times. And there was no way they could ever have any kind of permanent relationship.

So how could she even be *considering* having sex with him? All the years of being responsible, of doing what was expected of her, of being a *Rockwell* with all that meant, told her to go slow. To think long and hard before doing anything she might be sorry for later.

It was after eight by the time they reached the outskirts of Rockwell. Five minutes later Sabrina pulled into the parking lot of the motel.

She waited in the car while Gregg went in and registered and got his key. When he came back, he said, "I'm on the second floor in the back. The clerk said we can drive around."

Sabrina was glad her car couldn't be seen from the road, although she couldn't imagine that anyone she knew would be out here looking at the cars in the parking lot. This motel and the other two close to the interstate were mostly used by people passing through. Those who were staying in Rockwell generally stayed in town at the Rockwell Inn. She wished Gregg could be staying there, too, because it was a lovely place, and he would have enjoyed it, but she couldn't take that chance. If anyone were to see her with Gregg and mention it to her mother, well, it didn't bear thinking about.

There was a parking spot right next to the stairs leading up to the second level. Sabrina shivered as they climbed up.

"Cold?" He slipped his arm around her again.

"A little." But it wasn't the nippy air that made her shiver. It was the anticipation of what might happen...*would* happen if she wanted it.

This was madness, and she knew it. Nothing could ever come of this relationship. Gregg was Glynnis's twin. And Glynnis... Glynnis would forever be a name not spoken in her mother's presence, an existence not acknowledged. So how could Sabrina hope to have any kind of relationship with Gregg other than what was ahead of them tonight?

Suddenly her doubts overwhelmed her. If she had any sense at all, she'd tell Gregg she'd made a mistake. That as much as she liked him, and as attracted as she was to him, and as much as she wanted him, they couldn't go any further.

"What is it, Sabrina?" he asked. By now they had reached the doorway to his room.

She looked up. The moonlight had turned his hair to silver. "I—" She couldn't finish.

He bent down, brushing his lips over hers. "We don't have to do anything you don't want to do," he said gently. "If you want, I'll just drop my stuff, and we can go somewhere and have dinner. I'm happy simply to be with you."

And just like that, everything was all right again.

Sabrina put her arms around his waist and laid her cheek against his chest. His arms closed tightly around her. She could hear his heart beating in rhythm with her own.

I love him, she thought. *I don't care about tomorrow; I don't care about anything except today.*

"Let's go in," she said. She pulled back so she could see his face and he could see hers.

"Are you sure?"

"Yes, I'm sure."

For the first time in her life, she was going to do what her heart desired, no matter what the consequences.

Chapter Seven

The room looked like any other motel room. Impersonal and uninspired, with factory-outlet furniture and discount-house paintings. But it was clean and it was private, and once the door was shut behind them, it was the only world that mattered.

"Sabrina…" Gregg said.

His eyes were so blue. A bottomless ocean. She felt as if she were drowning in them.

He dropped his bag.

And opened his arms.

When he closed them around her, she knew she was where she belonged.

Afterward, she never remembered how they'd shed their clothes or how they'd taken the covers off the bed or even how they'd ended up in it.

All she knew was the need that had been building from the moment he'd arrived had escalated to the point that kisses were soon not enough.

And so their clothes were discarded, and the bed was uncovered, and then they were lying in it together, their legs and arms entwined. The feel of Gregg's hard body, with its angles and planes that were so different from her softness and curves, felt so good and so right. They fit together perfectly, as if they'd been made for each other.

Sabrina could feel the blood rushing through her veins as Gregg caressed and kissed her. Her insides felt like molten lava as her desire for him grew.

"Sabrina," he whispered, trailing kisses down her neck, to her breasts. "You're so beautiful."

She moaned and twined her hands through his hair as his lips moved lower, to her belly, then lower still. "I—I'm not beautiful."

"You're the most beautiful woman I ever saw."

Her breath caught as he parted her legs. When his tongue found her, she gasped and arched. Her heart thundered in her ears as a kaleidoscope of sensations exploded inside her.

Gregg held her fast until she stopped trembling. Only then did he enter her, pushing deep. She pulled him in as far as she could, loving the feel of him inside her.

As they began to move together, and her body once more started to stir, she twined her legs around him and gave herself up to the glorious feelings.

Yes, she thought, *yes.* This was what she'd wanted and needed. This connection, flesh to flesh, heart to heart. This was what her life had been missing.

She cried out when, with a final thrust, his life force spilled into her. Her body tightened around him as wave after wave of intense pleasure assaulted her.

Once their hearts calmed and their bodies cooled, he pulled her to him spoon fashion. Smoothing her hair back, he nuzzled her ear. "You're amazing," he whispered.

"No, I'm not."

"You are." He cupped her breast, idly stroking the nipple with his thumb. "Everything about you is amazing."

"You're embarrassing me."

He chuckled. "Get used to it."

Sabrina wanted to believe that she and Gregg could be together again, but she was afraid. She'd pushed aside her better judgment tonight and followed her heart. Where that would lead her, she didn't know.

They didn't talk after that. Instead, they made love again, slowly this time, and then they slept in each other's arms. The next morning, Gregg woke her with a kiss, and soon they were making love again. In fact, for most of the weekend, they spent their time in bed.

When they were hungry, they sent out for pizza or Gregg went for Chinese food. Sabrina was too nervous about anyone she knew seeing them together to risk going to any of the restaurants nearby. Gregg said he didn't mind. This way he had her all to himself.

"Besides," he said, laughing, "staying here does away with the need for clothes." Playfully he swatted her behind.

"Stop that," she said as the swat became a love pat, but she didn't push his hand away.

"Come here, woman." He pulled her onto his lap.

Sabrina sighed with pleasure.

All too soon, it was Sunday afternoon and time for Gregg to leave. Their goodbye kiss at the Akron-Canton airport was bittersweet.

"I'll come again as soon as I can," he said, holding her close.

Then, in a moment Sabrina knew she'd never forget, he whispered, "I love you. Everything will work out."

Sabrina's eyes filled with tears. "I love you, too."

They kissed again, a sweet kiss that expressed everything they felt. Seconds later, he was gone.

"Where were you this weekend?" Glynnis said. "I thought the conference was over on Friday."

"It was. I stopped off to visit a friend on the way back." Gregg knew she wanted to ask who the friend was. He was prepared if she did, although he didn't like lying to Glynnis. But he'd promised Sabrina he wouldn't say anything about the two of them to anyone until she was ready. He wondered what Glynnis would think about his involvement with Ben's daughter. Would it bother his twin? Or would she be happy for him?

"Oh."

"So why did you call? Did you need me for something?"

"No, I brought the kids to the restaurant for dinner Saturday night, and they were disappointed that you weren't there."

"I'm sorry. Bring them again sometime this week. If you come early I can probably have dinner with you."

"Okay. They'll like that."

"Hey, Gregg. Oh, sorry. I didn't know you were on the phone." Steve stood in the doorway to Gregg's office.

"That's okay. Listen, Glynnie, I've got to go. Let me know what night you're coming."

"I will."

After hanging up, Gregg dealt with Steve's question, then booted up his computer. Opening his e-mail program, he began to type.

FROM: Gregg Antonelli
TO: Sabrina March
Monday, 11/17, 9:30 a.m.

Dear Sabrina,
Hope it's okay to e-mail you at work. I tried calling you earlier, but Vicki said you were out on a story

and wouldn't be back until one. Since that's our busy time here at the restaurant, I decided to e-mail you instead.

Just wanted to tell you how much the weekend meant to me. I haven't been able to stop thinking about it or you. Do you have any idea how beautiful you are? And sexy. I can hear you now, saying you're not. Believe me, you are. If I wasn't afraid someone working for my Internet provider might be reading this, I'd write some X-rated stuff to prove it to you! <g>

Seriously, I can't wait to see you again. I wish I could come to Rockwell again this weekend, but it's impossible. It was a miracle I got away this past week. If it hadn't been for Igor I wouldn't have been able to. I told you about him, didn't I? We worked together for years, he's a real pro. He's retired now but he doesn't mind helping me out occasionally. I don't like to ask him too often, though, and someone's gotta be here, especially since I'm still having problems with my chef. I'll tell you about him the next time we talk.

Back to the problem at hand. Next week, I could come to Rockwell Wednesday night and drive back Thursday night. The only thing is, Thursday is Thanksgiving, which is why I'm able to get away. We don't open the restaurant on Thanksgiving. What do you think? Can you spend any time with me at all if I come? Or are you going to have to be with your mother all day? Let me know as soon as you can, okay?

Love,
Gregg

FROM: Sabrina March
TO: Gregg Antonelli
Monday, 11/17, 1:46 p.m.

Hi, Gregg,
Of course it's okay to e-mail me at work. In fact, it's the best way to get in touch with me. Your e-mail made me blush. X-rated! I can't imagine anyone less likely to be X-rated than me. In my high school yearbook they said I was the girl most likely to do the right thing. <g> You sure you've got the right girl?

I've been thinking about the weekend all morning, too. It was wonderful, and I can't wait to see you again, either, but Thanksgiving is going to be a problem. I can spend Wednesday night with you, but not Thursday. You don't know how much I wish I could just bring you to the house so you could spend the day with us, but you know that's impossible. How would I explain who you are? I'd have to lie, and I don't want to lie any more than is absolutely necessary. As it is, I feel terrible that I lied to my mother when she called me Friday night.

I'm so sorry about Thanksgiving and so disappointed. I imagine you won't want to come at all if all I can give you is Wednesday night.

Love,
Sabrina

FROM: Gregg Antonelli
TO: Sabrina March
Monday night, 11/17, 11:30 p.m.

Dear Sabrina,
I'm glad we talked. E-mail is great, but hearing your voice is better. Like I said, don't ever think it's not worth coming to see you if all we can have together is an evening. Even if all we have is an hour, it would still be worth it. So I'm coming. I'll let you know what time I'll be getting in. We'll have our own private Thanksgiving Wednesday night, and I'll go back Thursday morning. I don't want you to feel bad about this, either. By going home early, I'll be able to have dinner with Glynnis and the kids, so this is probably best all the way around. Talk to you tomorrow.
　Love,
Gregg

FROM: Sabrina March
TO: Gregg Antonelli
Tuesday, 11/18, 7:40 a.m.

Hi, Gregg,
Just got into the office and read your e-mail. Don't make a hotel reservation for Wednesday night. Instead, stay with me. Okay?
　I'm going to be tied up with meetings this morning, but I should be free this afternoon, so if you get a minute when lunch is over, call me.

Can't wait till next week.
   Love,
Sabrina

FROM: Gregg Antonelli
TO: Sabrina March
Tuesday, 11/18, 3:00 p.m.

Sabrina,
Sorry we missed each other when I called. Stay with you? Try to stop me! <g> Okay, we'll talk tonight.
   Love,
Gregg

FROM: Casey Hudson
TO: Sabrina March
Friday, 11/21, 2:02 p.m.

Hi, Sabrina,
I guess you got my message about my mom. I'm here now but spending most of my time at the hospital. If you want to reach me, call me on my cell phone, okay?

The doctors say the stroke was minimal, but she's still having trouble speaking, and she can't do much with her left arm. I don't know how long I'm going to have to stay in Florida, but I told Jack and Johnny not to expect me back before the end of the month. Thank God I have an understanding boss as well as a wonderful husband and son. Gil told me to take all the time I need.

Greta will get here later today, and Steve is coming tomorrow. I hate the reason, but I love that I'll get to spend some time with my siblings.

Write when you get a chance and tell me everything that's happening with you and Gregg.

Love,
Casey

FROM: Sabrina March
TO: Casey Hudson
Friday, 11/21, 10:43 p.m.

Hi, Casey,
Yeah, I got your message. What a bummer! Tell your mom I'm thinking about her and I'll add her to my prayer list. Why is it that the nicest people seem to have the worst luck? I mean, she's only been retired for six months. Is this fair? How's your dad holding up? It's so good that you and Greta and Steve could come, and I'm glad you're going to stay with her a while.

You asked about Gregg. Oh, Casey, he's the perfect man. I can't wait for you to meet him. He's coming to town again next week, on Wednesday night. He wanted to spend Thanksgiving together, but I just can't. I have to spend the day with my mother. If only I could tell her about him. If only this could be a normal relationship and I could take him home to meet her.

:::sigh:::

Well, wishing isn't going to change a thing, is it?

Sorry to dump on you. Keep me posted on your mom. Call me anytime if you need to talk.

Love ya,
Sabrina

FROM: Gregg Antonelli
TO: Sabrina March
Sunday night, 11/23, 11:12 p.m.

Hi!

Didn't want to call. I know you're asleep. Just wanted you to know I'll get to your place by five o'clock on Wednesday. Now I'm hitting the sack and plan to dream about you. X-rated, of course.
<g>

Love,
Gregg

FROM: Casey Hudson
TO: Sabrina March
Tuesday, 11/25, 1:13 p.m.

Sorry I haven't written, Sabrina. It's been hectic around here, but I think things will settle down soon. It looks like they're going to let Mom come home next week. She's doing so much better, it's like a miracle, really. We're so thankful.

I'll be dying to hear all about Thanksgiving.
TTYL,
Casey

FROM: Sabrina March
TO: Irene Loring
Tuesday, 11/25, 4:45 p.m.

Aunt Irene!
It was so great to hear from you. I couldn't believe it when I saw your name on an e-mail. See? Hell didn't have to freeze over for you to get computer literate. <g>

You asked about Mom. Except for concern about Dad's company—I'll tell you about that later—she seems to be doing much better. I was over there for dinner last night, and she was in the best spirits I've seen her in since Dad died. She actually laughed several times, and only once did she mention the scandal—her word, not mine.

Maybe her attitude has something to do with what's happening with Leland and Cecily Fox. It turns out they've separated, and I guess Leland told Mom that Cecily is filing for a divorce. Not that I think Mom is happy about Leland's problems…it's just that this new development has turned town gossip away from our family and in the direction of the Foxes.

About Dad's company. Mom and I have met with Bob Culberson and he's recommending that we sell. One of the big tour companies has made an offer, and it's a pretty good one. Mom is talking to Leland about it—I guess trying to determine if it would be a good move financially. If we don't sell, we'll have to hire a couple of people. I'll keep you posted.

You asked if you should come for Christmas. Selfishly, I wish you would. It would be great to have you and Uncle Robert and Jennifer here, because I am so dreading the holidays. I know they will be hard on Mom and, in turn, hard on me. But I hate for you to feel as if you have to come. I know you'd much rather be at home, and I'm sure Uncle Robert would. But you're such a sweetheart to offer. Maybe Mom and I should come to Savannah. What do you think about that?

Take care, Aunt Irene. Give my love to Uncle Robert and Jennifer and have a wonderful Thanksgiving.

Love you,
Sabrina

FROM: Irene Loring
TO: Sabrina March
Wednesday, 11/26, 9:00 a.m.

Sabrina, my dear, I think it's an excellent idea for you and Isabel to come to Savannah over the Christmas holidays. Your mother hates the winter weather, anyway, now that she can no longer ski, so she'd probably really enjoy the milder climate here. If you come, I'll plan all kinds of outings and festivities to keep her both occupied and distracted. Savannah is very much the party city during December, and I know your mother would enjoy meeting all our friends.

You know, I never dreamed how much I would

love this e-mail thing. It's so much fun! I've already got several correspondents listed in my address book. Why didn't I do this years ago? I should have listened to you and Jennifer.

Let me know about Christmas. If you're coming, you'd better decide quickly so you can get a good flight.

With love,
Aunt Irene

FROM: Sabrina March
TO: Casey Hudson
Thursday night, 11/27, 11:15 p.m.

Hi, Casey! Happy Thanksgiving. I just got home from Mom's. The day wasn't nearly as hard I expected it to be, mainly because Leland came for dinner and brought along his sister Carolee, who came in from New York to spend the weekend with him. Guess she feels sorry for him now that he's going through a divorce. Tell you the truth, I'm surprised he didn't go to New York instead of her coming here, but maybe she wanted to visit old friends. After all, she grew up here. Do you remember her? She looks exactly like him. Acts like him, too. She works on Wall Street, and she told some fascinating stories during dinner.

As always, Florence cooked a terrific dinner. We are so lucky to have her. I can't imagine how we'd manage if we didn't.

Casey, I'm in a bad way. Gregg was here yesterday, as you know, and we had such a wonderful time together. After he got here, we drove to Akron and went out to dinner at this fabulous restaurant where he knows the chef, then we went dancing at this little club. Then, of course, we came back here and...well, the rest is too personal to tell. Just let me say he's perfect. The perfect man. Everything I've ever dreamed about. Which is pretty scary, considering the odds against us.

I know, I know. Look on the bright side. Believe me, I'm trying.

I miss you. Hope you'll be coming home soon. Give my love to your family.

Sabrina

From: Gregg Antonelli
To: Sabrina March
Friday, 11/28, 3:00 p.m.

Hi, Sabrina. I'm stuffed from eating so much yesterday. How about you? I hope you had a good day with your mother. All the time I was at Glynnis's, I kept thinking about our own private Thanksgiving celebration Wednesday night. I'll probably be thinking about it every night until I see you again, and you give me something else to think about. <g>

I'm glad you decided to go to Savannah over the Christmas holidays. At first, I was disappointed I wouldn't get to see you, but it's not like we'd get to spend much time together anyway. We already know—from Thanksgiving—that the day itself is going to have to be spent with your mother, just as I need to be with Glynnis and the kids. This year will be really hard for them. Hard for all of us.

But I'll miss you.

Gotta run now. Did I tell you Joe is making noises about quitting? You know, much as I hate having to try to find a new chef, that guy has given me so much grief that if he does quit, I'm not going to lose any sleep over it. Besides, Igor says he heard a rumor that a chef we know—one who's really good—might be looking for a new position. So who knows? This could work out well.

I'll call you about ten tonight.

Love,

Gregg

FROM: Sabrina March
TO: Gregg Antonelli
Saturday, 11/29, 11:00 a.m.

Hi, Gregg. Well, I did it. I know you thought I should wait, but I decided to try to talk to my mother about Glynnis and the kids. It was a disaster. I should have known it would be. She put her hands over her ears and said she didn't want to hear anything about them...ever. She said as far as she was concerned, they don't exist.

I don't know. I get more discouraged every day. I had hoped that maybe, someday, she would accept the situation. But it doesn't look like that'll ever happen, because once my mother makes up her mind about something, that's it.

Write and tell me something good, okay?

Love,
Sabrina

FROM: Gregg Antonelli
TO: Sabrina March
Saturday, 11/29, 2:30 p.m.

Hey, sweet thing, cheer up! It's only been six weeks since your father died and less than that since your mother's known about his secret life. You can't expect her to get over a thing like that so soon. Give her time.

On another subject, can you manage to get away on Wednesday? Last time we were together you suggested that the next time I come to see you, we might spend the day at Chagrin Falls. Want to do that? I could drive in on Tuesday night and go back early Thursday morning. I've twisted Igor's arm, and he's agreed to come in and play boss for the day. Soon I won't have to bother him, because Steve is working out well. That kid catches on so fast, it's scary. I was kidding him today saying he must have plans to take over my job. It won't be long before he can fill in for me.

If you'd rather go in to Cleveland, that's fine, too. Your choice. If you decide on Cleveland, we can spend Tuesday night at one of the fancy downtown hotels and go to The Flats for dinner.

Sabrina, I never thought I'd feel this way about anyone. I want to shout it out to the whole world. I love you, and I want everyone to know it.

Gregg

FROM: Sabrina March
TO: Gregg Antonelli
Monday, 12/1, 10:00 a.m.

Dearest Gregg,

I'm glad we decided on Cleveland tomorrow night. It's going to be lots of fun. You know I love you, too. I worry, though. I don't like this sneaking around, yet the thought of bringing our relationship into the open is terrifying. After the way my mother acted when I tried to talk to her about Glynnis, I know exactly how she would react to my relationship with you.

I feel guilty. I'm all she has, and I understand how she must feel. If my father had lived a normal life and there was no betrayal, she would have moved on quickly, I think, because I don't believe she truly loved my father. I think, for her, it's mostly her pride that won't allow her to let go of this.

I wish I knew what to do. It's bad enough that he betrayed her. How can I betray her, too?

Love,
Sabrina

Sabrina looked at what she'd written. Maybe she should delete that last part. Maybe Gregg didn't want to hear about her fears. Maybe he thought she was a coward.

But if they were to have any kind of real relationship, it was important to be honest.

Before she could change her mind, she hit Send.

Chapter Eight

"Sabrina, your mother's on line three."

"Thanks, Vicki." She punched the blinking button. "Mom? Hi."

"Good morning, Sabrina. I'm sorry to bother you at work, but I just got a call from Bob Culberson. The Kenyon people? The ones who made the offer to buy the company? They've retracted their offer."

"Why?"

"I don't know. I really don't care. Frankly, I think it's just as well. I'm not sure their offer *was* the best we can do. And I told Bob that."

"Mom, you didn't criticize Bob, did you? He's worked so hard since Dad died."

"No, Sabrina, I am not stupid. I know he's worked

hard. I just think he's so anxious to get out from under that he made the Kenyon offer seem better than it really was. At any rate, he's going to put more feelers out. Apparently Greenlee Tour Company expressed an interest in buying March Tours a year ago. Bob said he'd give Marcus Greenlee a call and see if he might still be interested. I also called Leland and he's going to do some inquiring on our behalf, as well.''

"Good. I guess that means you've made up your mind to sell?''

Her mother sighed, the sound clearly audible over the phone. "Since there is no family member to take over, and since Bob clearly wants out, I think selling is the sensible way to go.''

Sabrina was relieved. She thought selling was the sensible way to go, too, but she hadn't expected her mother to agree.

"Thank goodness we don't have this problem with the newspaper. Although, if you don't hurry up and get married and have an heir, we may face the same thing someday.''

Sabrina closed her eyes. She didn't trust herself to answer.

"And that brings me to the other reason I called. I wanted to invite you for dinner tomorrow night,'' her mother added in a not-so-subtle segue. "Frances Lucas's nephew recently moved to town. I told you about him. John Braley. He's a cardiologist. Joining Cal Redmond's practice. Anyway, he doesn't know many young people yet. We thought you might like to introduce him around.''

"Mom, I'm sorry, but I can't come tomorrow night. I've already got plans.''

"Surely you could change them, whatever they are. John is a very attractive young man, Sabrina. I particularly wanted you to meet him first." The implication was that John Braley would not last long on the singles scene.

"I'm very sorry to disappoint you, but I can't change my plans."

The silence stretched for so long Sabrina almost said something else. But she stopped herself in time. There was no reason to feel defensive. This was a last-minute invitation on her mother's part. Sabrina had no obligation to accept.

"You know, Sabrina," her mother said stiffly, "I don't ask you for many things, and when I do, I expect to receive some consideration from you."

Sabrina counted to ten. Then she answered more patiently and gently than she felt. "I know that, and I'd come if I could, but I can't cancel my date. It's important to me."

"Well, this is important to me."

Sabrina resolutely kept silent. Finally her mother said, "Tell me this. Is this engagement you can't break with a man?"

"Yes, it is."

"Have you been seeing him long?"

"No, not long."

"Who is he?"

"Look, Mom, please don't get mad, but I'm not ready to talk about him yet. Our…relationship is too new. It may lead to nothing. So I'd rather not discuss it until there's something to discuss."

"I see. Well, I won't pretend I'm not disappointed, because I am. But if you don't want to confide in me, I won't try to force you."

"Mom…"

"You *are* still planning to come over on Saturday to help me go through your father's study?"

"Yes, of course I am."

"Fine. I'll see you then."

After the conversation with her mother, Sabrina felt unsettled for hours. Her mother's reaction to the information that Sabrina was seeing someone told her everything she needed to know about what she would think when she found out who that someone was.

Sabrina had been right to begin with.

There was no way she could ever have any kind of permanent relationship with Gregg.

Not if she wanted to continue to have one with her mother.

FROM: Glynnis Antonelli
TO: Sabrina March
Thursday, 12/4, 12:45 p.m.

Hi, Sabrina,
I have a few minutes left on my lunch hour and

thought I'd just send you off a quick note. I'm so glad Gregg thought to give you my e-mail address and that you wrote. Even if we can't see each other in person, at least we can keep in touch.

Everything is fine with us. Michael lost one of his front teeth, and he's so proud. <g> Olivia thought it was cool, too, (her word, not mine). They mention you often, especially Michael. His teacher told me that on the last show-amd-tell day, he told the class about his big sister. The teacher was (naturally) curious, and I evaded the truth by telling her you were Ben's daughter from his first marriage. Actually, I guess that *is* the truth.

You asked about my job. At first it was hard to get back into the groove, and I hated having to put Olivia into day care, but she really loves the nursery school. She's made friends and adores her teacher (Miss Sweet)—don't you *love* the name? So descriptive. You should see this girl. She looks about seventeen, although I know for a fact she's twenty-three and has a degree in Early Childhood Education, and she really is the sweetest thing with freckles across her turned-up nose <g> and sparkling green eyes. I can see why Olivia loves her so much. Anyway, the situation has worked out fine. And my schedule is arranged so that I'm through for the day in time to pick up Michael at school.

Well, better scoot. I have a one o'clock class. TTYS
   Love,
Glynnis

FROM: Sabrina March
TO: Glynnis Antonelli
Thursday, 12/4, 3:12 p.m.

Dear Glynnis,
I was so pleased to hear from you! I'm glad your
job is going well and that it's not as bad as you
thought it might be to go back to work. And it's
great that Olivia has settled into the nursery school
so well. And Miss Sweet sounds, well, *sweet*!
<g> Don't you think "sweet" is a horrible word,
though? I used to always be described as sweet,
and I hated it. I wanted to be thought of as strong
and smart. Sweet. Yuck. <g>

   Tell Michael his big sister is sending him something for his next show-amd-tell. It has to do with
rockets. I think he'll really like it. I'll figure out something to send to Olivia, too. I don't want her to feel
left out.

   Take care, Glynnis, and keep in touch. Give the
kids a kiss and hug from me.

   Love,
Sabrina

FROM: Gregg Antonelli
TO: Sabrina March
Thursday, 12/4, 5:15 p.m.

Darling Sabrina,
I've been thinking about you ever since I got back

home. I keep picturing you in that big bed at the hotel, how sexy you looked in that lace nightgown I gave you. I knew that shade of blue would look good on you. You're one sexy lady. Have I told you that before? If not, I should have. I keep remembering all the things we did in that bed. Better stop right there... I'm getting hot. <g> When I talk this way, do I embarrass you? I love to see you blush. I didn't know there were any women out there who still knew *how* to blush!

You asked me about Lynn. When we were seeing each other, I thought I loved her, but I never felt about her what I feel about you. When I'm with you, nothing else seems to matter. Not the restaurant, not anything. You're the most important thing in the world to me, Sabrina. I'd do anything for you.

Some of the guys here at the restaurant have been ragging me. They know I'm seeing somebody, and they're all curious about who it is. Janine—you remember her, don't you? She's the night hostess—pretty, with blond hair. Anyway, she keeps saying I'm smiling too much.

Ah, hell, I'd better sign off. I'm starting to sound like an idiot. Besides, the dinner hour is cranking up, and they might need help in the kitchen.

I can't wait to see you again. What day would be good next week? Could you stay overnight in

Akron? I know you feel freer when we're not in Rockwell.

Always remember that I love you.

Gregg.

FROM: Sabrina March
TO: Gregg Antonelli
Thursday, 12/4, 7:00 p.m.

Dear Gregg,
Yes, you're embarrassing me!!! And yes, I blush when I read things like what you wrote. God, what if somebody else should see these posts?

And yet...okay, I'm going to be really, really honest with you. I like when you talk to me like that. And when we make love, I like when you whisper certain things in my ear. God, now I'm blushing *again*. And I'm wiggling in my chair!

Gotta run. Call me later. I'll wait up. We can have phone sex. <bg>

Love you,
Sabrina

FROM: Sabrina March
TO: Gregg Antonelli
Thursday, 12/4, 11:50 p.m.

Dear Gregg,
It's almost midnight. We just hung up, and I didn't want to break the connection. I wish...well, you know what I wish. Right now I just hope nothing

ever changes. I hope we can be like this, just the two of us, separate from everyone else, in our own world, forever.

Is that possible?

I'm scared. I love you.

Sabrina

Sabrina sat back on her heels and wiped perspiration off her face with the sleeve of her sweatshirt. She and her mother had been sorting through her father's desk and files since nine o'clock that morning. It was now after three, and they were only about halfway done.

"Let's quit for the day," she said, looking at her mother who had long ago become weary and sat at the window that overlooked the side yard. "We can do the rest of this tomorrow after church. I'll bring some old clothes with me so I won't have to go back to my apartment."

"All right," her mother agreed. "I believe I'll go and lie down for a while, then. Are you planning to stay for dinner?"

Sabrina bit her lip. "Um, no, but I can, if you want me to."

"No, that's all right. Don't worry about me." Her tone suggested long-suffering.

"But I *do* worry about you, Mom. Tell you what. I have some errands to run, so I'll go and do them now. Then I'll stop home and shower and change, and I'll be back here about seven to have dinner with you. Okay?''

Now that she'd gotten her way, Isabel smiled happily.

Before Sabrina left, she sought out Florence, who was in the kitchen, to say goodbye. "I'm coming back for dinner, so if you'd like to take the evening off, you can."

Florence smiled at her. "Thank you, dear. I appreciate the offer, but I'm fine."

"You're sure? I don't want you to wear yourself out tending Mother."

"Don't worry about me, Sabrina. If I need help, I'll tell you."

"You promise?" Florence was in her fifties, and although she was a healthy, strong woman, Sabrina knew the full-time care of her mother was a demanding and exhausting job.

"I promise. Now you go on. You look tired."

"I am tired."

"Sabrina, this isn't any of my business, but *you're* the one I worry about. You've got a lot riding on your shoulders right now."

You don't know the half of it. "I'm okay."

"You know," Florence said thoughtfully, "maybe we should think about hiring someone else to help out here. That way, you'd be freer and wouldn't have to stop by so many times a week and take your mother so many places."

"What kind of person were you thinking of?"

"A companion for your mother. Someone who could take her places and entertain her."

The thought was very tempting, but Sabrina had a feeling her mother would never agree. Still, it was something to think about. "I'd have to present the idea in just the right way."

Florence smiled. She understood what Sabrina hadn't said.

As Sabrina let herself out, she saw that a light snow had begun to fall. It was the first snowfall of the year. For some reason, seeing it made her feel sad. *I'm so tired of being pulled two ways.*

Something's got to give soon, she thought. Either she had to stop seeing Gregg, or she had to bite the bullet and tell her mother about him, no matter what the cost.

FROM: Glynnis Antonelli
TO: Sabrina March
Sunday, 12/7, 1:00 p.m.

Dear Sabrina,
I know you said you couldn't come back to Ivy, and I understand why, truly I do. And I wouldn't ask this of you if it didn't mean so much to Michael. If you say no, I'll understand and I'll try to explain it to him so that he understands, too.

Here's the deal: his class is having "what my dad does" day next week on Friday. He asked his teacher if he could bring his big sister to class instead because she works at a newspaper and he doesn't have a dad to bring. I don't know how he got this idea. When he first mentioned this, I thought he would bring Gregg, but he's adamant that he wants you. So I told Gregg about this, and he suggested that I ask you. So I'm asking.

Otherwise, hope all is going well. I'm busier than I've been in years. I really like teaching. It's so much fun at this level, because mostly the students really want to be here. That's not true of all colleges, but community colleges attract students who want an education more than most. I have one student—his name is Sam Donnelly—who is so talented. He's like a sponge (I know that's a cliché, but it's true). He absorbs everything I show him and then does it better. Right now he's working in pastels, and it's amazing what he can do with color. It's just such a pleasure seeing him get better and better.

But I'm probably boring you. Let me know about the Career Day thing. And Sabrina, I really will understand if you feel you can't come.

Warmly,
Glynnis

FROM: Gregg Antonelli
TO: Sabrina March
Sunday, 12/7, 2:30 p.m.

Sabrina,
I know you're at your mother's today and probably won't be back to read this until tonight, but I wanted

to give you a heads-up. Glynnis is going to ask you about coming to Michael's school for Career Day.

I'll call you tonight. Will you be home?

Love,
Gregg

FROM: Sabrina March
TO: Gregg Antonelli
Sunday, 12/7, 6:06 p.m.

Gregg,
I just got home and read both Glynnis's and your message. No, I won't be home tonight. I'm going back to Mother's for dinner and probably won't be home before eleven. I'll call you then.

Love,
Sabrina

FROM: Sabrina March
TO: Glynnis Antonelli
Monday, 12/8, 8:30 a.m.

Dear Glynnis,
I would have called you yesterday, but I didn't get home until late. I didn't even have to think about this. Of course, I'll come for Michael's Career Day. Send me the particulars, and I'll make the arrangements.

And I wasn't bored hearing about your teaching and your students. Don't laugh, but I'd love to take one of your classes myself. Like those people who all feel they have a book in them, I've always seen myself as an artist. <g>

Tell Michael I'm thrilled he wants me!

See you soon,
Sabrina

FROM: Michael Arthur
TO: Sabrina March
Saturday, 12/13, 9:30 a.m.

Dear Sabrina,
My mom is writing this, but I'm telling her what to say. Thank you very much for coming and talking to my class about the newspaper. They liked it very much, and I liked it very much. When I get big, I want to work at a newspaper like you do.

Love,
Your brother Michael

PS: (Glynnis here) He hasn't stopped talking about your visit since you left. Sabrina, I can't tell you how much your coming meant to both of us, and I know your father is probably smiling up in heaven.

Love,
Glynnis

FROM: Gregg Antonelli
TO: Sabrina March
Saturday, 12/13, 12:01 p.m.

Dear Sabrina,
Well, you made several people very happy yester-

day. Michael is beaming, and Glynnis gets teary eyed every time she sees how happy he is. And of course, you know you made *me* happy. I wish I could have had you stay here with me, but as long as Steve is bunking in with me, that's impossible. He's planning to move out the first of January, though, so if you come to Ivy again after that, you won't have to stay in a hotel. The only part of your visit I didn't like was having to pretend we are just casual friends in front of Glynnis and having to say goodbye to you this morning.

You know, I've never kept secrets from her, and it's getting harder and harder all the time to keep this one.

Talk to you later...when the lunch crowd thins out. If it ever does. Guess I shouldn't complain. We're a success. Too bad success always comes with a price. <g>

Love you,
Gregg

FROM: Sabrina March
TO: Michael Arthur
Saturday, 12/13, 1:30 p.m.

Dear Michael,
I'm so glad your class enjoyed my visit. I enjoyed meeting them, too, and I really liked your teacher. You're a lucky boy to have such a nice school.
   Love,
Your sister, Sabrina

FROM: Sabrina March
TO: Glynnis Antonelli
Saturday, 12/13, 1:36 p.m.

Dear Glynnis,
I was so touched by Michael's note. I hope I can
live up to his hero (heroine?) worship. He and
Olivia are such sweet children. I was wondering…do you have any recent pictures of them that
I might have? I would love to have one of each to
carry in my wallet.

It was lovely to see you again, too. I think, in
other circumstances, we could be very good friends.
Love,
Sabrina

FROM: Sabrina March
TO: Gregg Antonelli
Sunday morning, 12/14, 9:25 a.m.

Hi, Gregg,
I tried to call you a few minutes ago, but I got your
voice mail. I begged off church this morning, and
my mother was upset with me. I placated her by
saying I'd come over early today (I'm leaving about
eleven) and we could go out for brunch. The Rockwell Lodge puts on a wonderful Sunday brunch. I
hope someday I can take you there.

I should never have told my mother I was seeing
someone. Now she constantly asks me questions
about you, and it's hard telling her only so much

and not the rest. I am so tired of lying. I wish I could see a way out, but right now, I can't. Sometimes I think, just tell her and be done with it. But when I'm with her, I feel so bad and I just can't hurt her that way. What are we going to do?

I'm feeling very down today, as I'm sure you can tell. I'll call you after I get home tonight.

I love you.
Sabrina

FROM: Gregg Antonelli
TO: Sabrina March
Sunday, 12/14, midnight

Dear Sabrina,
I'm glad we got a chance to talk today, and I hope you're feeling better. Things are going to work out. I'm sure of it. Your mother will get stronger as time goes on, and I love you enough to wait. Not forever, of course. I'm not getting any younger, and if we're going to have half a dozen kids, we'd better get started fairly soon, don't you think?

You'll know when the time is right to tell her. Just hang in there. Everything's going to be okay. I promise.

All my love,
Gregg

Chapter Nine

"Gregg! Gregg! You've got to come. There's a crisis in the kitchen!"

Gregg, who had been sitting at his desk writing checks, jumped up. Maggie stood in the doorway to his office. Even her dark, corkscrew curls looked agitated, as if they were going to burst away from the headband she used to keep them out of her face.

"What's wrong?"

She rolled her eyes. "It's Joe."

Gregg swore. "What now?"

"He's gone on strike."

"On strike!"

"Yes."

"What the hell happened?"

"Table four sent back the osso buco, saying it had a funny taste. Joe had a fit, said the osso buco was perfect, that the customer wouldn't know good food if he fell over it."

Gregg swore again.

"Anyway, he wouldn't give Chris another plate, and Chris got furious. One thing led to another, and now Joe says he isn't going to work under these conditions where smart-assed waiters think they can tell him what to do and how to do it."

By now they'd reached the double swing doors that led to the kitchen. Pushing through so hard the doors banged against the inside walls, Gregg charged over to Joe, who sat up on the farthest stainless steel countertop smoking a cigarette.

"Just what the hell do you think you're doing?" Gregg roared. He yanked the cigarette out of Joe's hand and crushed it beneath his heel. Smoking was forbidden in the kitchen, and this was the first time anyone had broken the rule since it had been instituted.

"What does it look like I'm doing?" Joe countered insolently.

Gregg spoke through gritted teeth. "This is the lunch hour. We've got a full house out there. No one sits in this kitchen during meal times."

Joe sneered. "Then I'd say you've got a serious problem, 'cause I'm not moving." He stuck one clog-shod foot out and studied it.

"That's where you're wrong. Now you'd better

listen and listen good, because I'm only going to say this once. You've got to the count of ten to get up off your ass and get back to work.''

"Or what?"

"Or you're fired."

At Gregg's ultimatum, everything in the kitchen went still. Work stopped, and Gregg could feel everyone holding their breath.

"It's your funeral, hotshot," Joe said. "I never liked you or this job, anyway." And with that, he hopped down from the counter, removed his apron and threw it on the floor. "Don't think you're gonna get out of paying me what you owe me. I'm not leaving until I have my check. And you'd better not try to stiff me…'' He let the threat go unfinished.

"I always pay what I owe."

Without looking to see if Joe was following him, Gregg strode out.

Joe was right behind him as Gregg entered his office. Silently Gregg wrote out a check and handed it to Joe. Joe stared at it for a moment. Then, with a sneer, he folded it and put it in his wallet.

Very glad he'd never given Joe a key to the place, Gregg followed him outside, making sure Joe climbed on his motorcycle and left the premises. As soon as the chef was out of sight, Gregg headed back to the kitchen.

Six pairs of eyes stared at him when he entered. Calmly Gregg said, "Don't just stand there. Let's get busy. Maggie, you're temporarily our chef. I'll do sous-chef honors. Steve, you help Maggie. Just do whatever she tells you to do. Everybody else, get back to your normal duties.''

Gregg walked over to the sink and washed his hands. Then he took a clean apron out of the linen drawer and wrapped it around him.

''What should I do about the customer who's waiting for another osso buco?'' Chris asked.

''I'll go out and talk to him. Which table?''

''Number twelve, party of two.''

Gregg headed out to the main dining room. Two men in expensive-looking suits were at table twelve. One of them—a typical Young Turk type—was angrily tapping his manicured fingernails on the tabletop. Gregg didn't recognize either of the men, which was too bad. Regular customers would be easier to deal with.

''Hello,'' he said when he reached their table. ''I'm Gregg Antonelli, the owner.''

Both men murmured greetings. The angry one looked as if he was going to blow any minute. The other one, who had a half-eaten plate of Chicken Marsala in front of him, looked embarrassed and wouldn't meet Gregg's eyes.

''I apologize for the osso buco,'' Gregg said, turning to the angry one. ''Unfortunately, I can't offer you another, but I can give you anything else on the menu that you'd like, and to make it up to you, both your meals will be complimentary today.''

After a moment, the anger faded from the man's

eyes. He nodded. "In that case, I'll have what he's eating." He gestured toward his lunch partner's plate.

Gregg smiled. "Excellent choice. It'll be out in just a couple of minutes. Now, would you like a bottle of wine to go with your pasta? With my compliments, of course."

Crisis averted, Gregg returned to the kitchen, gratified to see that everyone was now working busily. Maggie smiled at him as he began chopping onions. "You did the right thing," she said. "And we'll be fine. Don't worry."

He smiled back. "I'm not worried. I'm relieved."

For the next two hours, Gregg was so busy he didn't have time to think. By the time the lunch crowd was gone and the immediate crisis over, he realized Maggie had done a credible job of filling in for Joe and they'd only had to remove two items from the menu.

But dinner would be another story. There were items on the dinner menu that Maggie had never made, and it would be asking a lot of her to learn under this kind of emergency.

"Can you guys handle things on your own for a while?" he asked.

They all said they could, so Gregg headed for his office where he promptly put in a call to Igor.

"Don't tell me you want to go see that girlfriend of yours again?" Igor said. "My advice is to marry the girl if you can't stay away from her."

"That's not why I'm calling. I had to fire Joe. He walked out two hours ago."

"From what you told me, it was just a matter of time, anyway."

"Yeah, but now I need a chef, like, right away."

"Let me make a few calls for you."

"I was hoping you'd say that."

After hanging up, Gregg sat for a moment, thinking. He wasn't sorry he'd fired Joe. The man had been causing too much trouble for too long. His presence had put a strain on the entire staff. Still, being without a versatile chef of Joe's caliber for any length of time would hurt the business because Maggie, as good as she was, had limited experience. It would take her time to get up to speed, and time was a luxury they didn't have with the busy Christmas season practically upon them. Gregg needed to find a good, experienced chef right away.

Sometimes Gregg wondered if owning his own place was worth it. Last year he'd been offered a job with a high quality chain. They'd wanted him to take over as their general manager. The pay was excellent, the benefits good, and he would have had more or less normal hours. Yet he hadn't even considered doing it, even though he knew he could have sold Antonelli's and made a tidy profit.

The phone interrupted his thoughts.

"It's your sister on line one," Janine said.

Gregg punched the button. "Hi. What's up?"

"I'm calling to ask a favor. Could you possibly

pick up the kids from school today? The dean has
called a meeting and I have to go.'' When Glynnis
returned to work, she could no longer car pool.

''Sure. What time?''

''Michael will be out at three, and Livvy can be
picked up anytime up until six, although I usually
get her right after getting Michael.''

''I can go get them, no problem, but we're in a
real bind here today, so I won't be able to stay with
them. What time are you going to be free?''

''The meeting should be over by four. Tell you
what, if you can get Michael and take him back to
the restaurant with you, I'll call Livvy's school and
tell her I'm coming later, then I'll swing by there and
get Michael.''

''Okay. That'll work.''

''Thank you. I'll see you later.''

Gregg hung up, then eyed the open checkbook. He
hadn't finished paying the bills and it didn't look as
if he was going to have time to do them today.
Sweeping everything into his top desk drawer, he
buzzed Janine. ''I've got to leave for about thirty
minutes. If Igor Rudinsky calls, tell him I'll call him
back as soon as I return.''

''Okeydoke.''

Fifteen minutes later, Gregg stood outside Michael's school. Within moments, the school bell
sounded, followed by an onslaught of kids streaming
out the front door.

''Uncle Gregg!'' Michael had spied him.

"Hey, tiger. How's it goin'?" Gregg put his hand on Michael's shoulder.

"Okay." Michael grinned, looking around. "Where's my mom?"

"She had a meeting, so I'm picking you guys up today."

"Cool."

Gregg laughed. It always amused him to hear Michael say things like "cool." "We're going to the restaurant for a while, okay?"

"Yeah! Can I help in the kitchen?"

"I don't know. We're pretty busy today. We'll see when we get there, okay?"

"Okay."

Michael was such a good kid, Gregg thought, not for the first time. He rarely argued when told no, which Gregg knew from listening to his married buddies who had kids wasn't the norm. He smiled. Livvy, on the other hand, would probably drive Glynnis crazy, because that little girl was one stubborn cookie.

As if he'd read Gregg's mind, Michael said, "Are we gonna get Livvy?"

"Nope. Your mom will pick her up when she gets out of her meeting."

By now they'd reached Gregg's Ford Explorer truck and Gregg opened the back door so Michael could climb in. After adjusting the seat belt for him, Gregg got into the truck himself. A minute later they were on their way.

When they walked into the kitchen, everyone made a fuss over Michael. Joni, the pastry chef, set him to work stirring egg whites that had already been whipped into a froth. She winked at Gregg, silently saying it was no problem.

"Thanks," Gregg said. "I'll be in my office if you need me."

"We'll be fine."

"You're coming back to help with the salads, aren't you?" Maggie asked.

"I'll be back in a few minutes. Just need to check on something first."

Gregg was pleased to find out that Igor had called while he was gone.

"I hope you've got good news for me," he said when he got Igor on the line.

"Maybe. Do you remember Mark Carducci?"

"Yeah, sure. Assistant chef at Frenchie's."

"He's got a good rep, and he's on the market." Igor went on to tell Gregg what Mark Carducci had been doing recently. "Are you interested?"

"Yes, of course. He sounds great."

"Okay, then. Bud McIntyre gave me his number."

"Great. I'll call him right now."

"You want me to come and help out for a few days?"

"I don't want to get Ludmilla mad at me."

"She doesn't care. Her sister's coming to spend a few days, anyway. They'll probably be glad to have me out of their hair. Hey, Ludmilla," he yelled.

"You care if I go help Gregg out for a few days?"
A few seconds later, he chuckled. "She said good
riddance."

Gregg laughed. "Then I can definitely use you."

"I'll be there in the morning."

As soon as they'd hung up, Gregg called the number Igor had given him for Mark Carducci. Luck was
with him, and Carducci answered the phone on the
third ring.

"Mark, hi. It's Gregg Antonelli. I don't know if
you remember me but—"

"Sure, I remember you. How are you?"

After a few minutes of small talk, Gregg got to
the point and explained his situation. "I know it's
not Chicago, but I think you'd like working here. Are
you interested?"

"Yeah, I am."

They talked awhile more and made arrangements
for Mark to come for a visit and interview two days
later.

When Gregg hung up, he felt as though a load had
been taken off his shoulders.

He was smiling when he went back to the kitchen.
All they had to do was get through tonight, because
tomorrow Igor would be here, and the next day—if
all went right—maybe they'd have a new chef.

"How's my buddy doing?" he asked Michael,
who was now happily rolling out pie crust dough.

"Leftovers," Joni said sotto voce. She grinned at
Michael. "He's a great little helper."

A few minutes later, Glynnis walked in, and Michael proudly showed her his handiwork.

"Wow," she said. "I'm going to have to put you to work in the kitchen at home." She smiled at Gregg. "Thanks, bro. I owe you one."

"My pleasure."

Glynnis chatted with the rest of the kitchen personnel for a while, then said to Michael, "I know you probably don't want to, but it's time to go, honey. Livvy's waiting for us to pick her up."

Michael frowned for a couple of seconds, then brightened when Joni said she'd put his dough in a plastic bag for him, and he and his sister could roll it out when they got home. "After you get it rolled out, tell your mom to spread butter over it, then sprinkle cinnamon and sugar on it, then roll it up like a jelly roll, then cut it into pieces to bake it."

"*Okay!*" Michael said, grinning. "Did'ya hear that, Mom?"

"I sure did," Glynnis said, smiling her thanks at Joni.

Gregg walked Glynnis and Michael out to her car.

"We haven't seen much of you lately," she said.

"I know. I'm sorry. I've been really busy."

Glynnis nodded thoughtfully. "Sure there's nothing you want to tell me?"

"Like what?"

"Like, are you seeing someone? You seem to be gone an awful lot." She grinned. "An inquiring twin wants to know."

Gregg shrugged as nonchalantly as he could. He didn't want to lie outright.

"Well, are you or aren't you?" Glynnis pressed.

"Okay, I am. But I'm not ready to talk about her."

Glynnis raised her eyebrows. "Really? That sounds serious."

"What makes you say that?"

"If it wasn't serious, you'd be telling me everything."

Gregg laughed uncomfortably. "I don't get your reasoning."

"That's because you're a man."

"Every time you say something totally illogical and I call you on it, you say I don't understand because I'm a man."

Glynnis laughed. "Well, it's true."

Gregg shook his head. "Women."

"All right, I'm not going to bug you about her right now. But I'm dying to know who she is and what she's like. And I intend to find out. So consider yourself warned."

As soon as Sabrina got home Monday night, she put in a call to Gregg.

"Hi," he said, "this is a pleasant surprise. I didn't expect to hear from you tonight."

"I'm sorry to bother you at work, but I had to talk to you."

"Is something wrong?"

"Oh, Gregg. I'm sorry. I know you're probably

sick of me, and I know you told me not to worry, but I can't help it. I don't know. Today everything— all the lying, all the sneaking around, all the hiding— it just seemed to pile up on me. I hate it! And the trouble is, I don't see any end in sight." She was close to tears. "What's going to happen to us?"

"I love you, Sabrina. You know that. I want to marry you, build a life with you, have children with you. I thought that's what you wanted, too."

"I want that more than anything."

"But?"

"But I don't see how it can ever happen."

"If you want it to happen, it will. All you have to do is tell your mother the truth."

"You make it sound so easy."

"I know it won't be easy. Look, you're leaving for Savannah on Tuesday."

"Yes."

"I have to be here Saturday, but why don't I come to Rockwell on Sunday? We'll go and talk to your mother together. Then the two of you will have the holidays with your aunt—who you said is always supportive—and maybe by the time you come back home, your mother will be reconciled to everything."

Oh, God. Just the thought of facing her mother and telling her the truth made Sabrina shiver. "Gregg."

"You know you have to tell her eventually. Why not just get it over with? This is the perfect time."

"I don't know."

"Sabrina, either you love me or you don't. You do love me, don't you?"

"You know I love you."

"Then you'll face your mother and you'll tell her about us. I know you don't want to hurt her," he added more gently, "and I admire you for it. But Sabrina, you can't live your entire life for your mother. I think you know that."

Sabrina also knew Gregg wasn't going to be patient forever. By putting off the confrontation, she was running the risk of losing him. She took a deep breath. "Okay. Come on Sunday."

After they hung up, she started to cry. At that moment, she hated her father. Why had he done this to them? And yet, if he hadn't, she would never have met Gregg.

Please, God, she prayed, *let it be okay. I know I'm asking for a miracle, but if you make it okay with my mother, I'll never ask you for anything again.*

Gregg couldn't get Sabrina out of his mind after their phone conversation. He hoped she didn't get cold feet about them talking to her mother on Sunday, although it wouldn't surprise him if she did. This was going to be very hard for her. He knew that. But if they were to have a future together, it had to be done.

"Man, you look like your dog just died."

Gregg looked up to see Steve standing in the doorway. He smiled. "I don't have a dog."

Steve walked in and plopped down in the chair that was wedged between the corner of Gregg's desk and the filing cabinet. He crossed his long legs. "I wanted to ask you something."

"Shoot."

"Do you have any rules against fraternizing here?"

Gregg raised his eyebrows. "Who's caught your eye? Janine? Or Maggie?" Both women were in their twenties and both were very pretty.

Steve smiled. "Maggie."

"Does she share your interest?"

"Yeah. I think so."

"This is kind of touchy. I mean, I don't have a problem with you dating someone who works here, but what happens if it doesn't work out? I'd sure hate to lose Maggie because she's pissed off at you."

Steve's smile faded. "Does that mean you don't want me dating her?"

Gregg sighed. "No. Just be careful, okay? Maggie's a key employee, plus she's a really nice girl. I don't want her getting her heart broken."

"I know. But don't worry. If anything happens, *I'll* go."

Gregg smiled. "I don't want to lose you, either."

After Steve left, Gregg rubbed his head. Did life ever run smoothly? he wondered. And yet…if it did, if nothing exciting ever happened, if you never had any problems, life would probably be too boring to stand.

He thought a moment or two more, then picked up the phone and punched in Sabrina's number. When she said hello, Gregg could immediately tell she'd been crying.

"I know I told you I had to be here Saturday night," he said, "but I've decided you're more important than any problems I might be having with the restaurant. I'm coming to Rockwell Saturday right after the lunch crowd thins out. I'll be there no later than four. I'll book us a room in Akron for the night. Let's plan to have dinner at Christina's Place, then we'll go dancing at Star's like we did before."

"Really?"

"Really."

"Gregg, I love you. I do. And…and I can do what I have to do on Sunday."

"I love you, too. I'll see you Saturday."

After Gregg's call Monday night, Sabrina felt an almost eerie sense of calm. The decision had been made, the die was cast. They were going to face her mother together on Sunday, and from then on she would not have to hide their relationship.

For better or worse, the truth would be out.

"That was a wonderful dinner," Sabrina said, sitting back with a sigh.

"Yeah, Christina's a terrific chef."

Sabrina picked up her wineglass and drank the last few drops. "The wine was wonderful, too." She looked at Gregg, thinking how handsome he looked in his collarless black shirt under a charcoal jacket.

They had started out the evening by checking into the Hilton—Gregg had booked a luxury suite—where they'd made leisurely love, then shared a shower. Afterward, they'd dressed—Sabrina in her favorite short black crepe dress with the ruffled hemline, and Gregg in gray slacks and the black shirt.

Soon they would leave the restaurant and go to Star's, the little club they discovered when they'd first begun seeing each other. Sabrina knew they'd dance close together, anticipating the moment when they'd leave and go back to the hotel where they'd cuddle together in their big bed and try not to think about anything else but how much they loved each other.

But it didn't happen quite that way.

They did go to Star's, and they did dance close together, and they did go back to the hotel. But before they could get into bed, Sabrina's cell phone rang. She almost didn't answer it, but caller ID showed her mother's cell phone number. Since it was after one in the morning, she knew it must be an emergency.

"It's my mother. I have to take it."

Gregg nodded.

"Hello?" she said.

"Sabrina?"

It wasn't her mother. It was Florence.

"Florence? What is it? Has something happened?"

"I tried to call you earlier, but you didn't answer."

Sabrina had turned her phone off during dinner and even though it had been on at Star's, she'd left it at the table when they were dancing. "I'm sorry. I was out for the evening."

"Your mother fell earlier tonight. She didn't wait for me to help her into bed, and somehow, she lost her balance and fell. She's broken her right arm."

"Oh no!"

"We're at the hospital. They've just set the bone and put the arm in a cast."

"Oh, no," Sabrina said again. Since the accident that had taken the use of her legs, Sabrina's mother had relied on her arms more than ever. Without the use of her right arm, she would be virtually helpless to do anything on her own.

"They've given her something for pain, and because of her paralysis, they're going to keep her overnight. I'll stay, but I thought you would like to know."

Sabrina nodded. Realizing Florence couldn't see her, she said, "Thank you, Florence. I—I'll get there as soon as I can."

"All right. And Sabrina? Maybe now would be a good time to find someone to come and help me."

"What happened?" Gregg said as Sabrina disconnected the call.

"My mother fell. She broke her arm." She finished explaining what Florence had told her and was grateful when Gregg understood without being told that she had to go home right away.

They didn't talk much as they drove back to Rockwell. When they got there, Gregg asked if she wanted to go home first or if she wanted him to drop her off at the hospital.

"Let's go to my apartment. I'll change clothes, and then I'll go see her."

"Okay."

She wondered what he was thinking. She was afraid to ask. When they reached her apartment, he took out her overnight bag but left his in the car.

"Aren't you going to stay over?"

He shook his head. "You'll be at the hospital all night."

"Oh, Gregg, I'm so sorry. You know—"

"I know," he interrupted. His smile was weary. "I thought about this all the way back. I think it'd be a good idea if we cool things for a while."

Sabrina's heart skipped. "Cool things?" she echoed. "Wh-what are you saying?"

He put his hands on the sides of her face. His voice was gentle as he answered. "Look, I love you. Nothing's going to change that. But seeing each other like this, it's too hard on both of us. For a while, at least until you feel you can openly acknowledge me and our relationship, I think it'll be easier if we don't see each other." Then he kissed her mouth softly. "Call me tomorrow and let me know how she is, okay?"

Sabrina nodded mutely. She told herself not to cry.

But her eyes blurred with tears as she watched him get back in his car and drive away.

I love you, he'd said. *Nothing's going to change that.*

So why did Sabrina feel as if she would never see him again?

Chapter Ten

The next few days were a nightmare for Sabrina. They had to cancel the trip to Savannah. There was no way they could go, not unless Florence went with them to help, and she had made plans to spend the holidays with her sister's family in Tucson. Sabrina simply didn't have the heart to ask Florence to change her plans, too.

Just before leaving, Florence said, "Maybe instead of hiring someone permanent to help out here, you could get temporary help from one of those nursing agencies. That way, nothing definite has to be decided immediately."

"That's a good idea, Florence."

But when Sabrina broached the subject of hiring a

nurse or a nurse's aide, Isabel adamantly said she wouldn't hear of it. "We'll be fine," she insisted.

"Mother," Sabrina said firmly, "you need someone to help you all the time now, at least until that arm heals. And I can see, just from the few days I've been here, how exhausting it is for one person to do everything. If *I'm* exhausted, then Florence is going to be overwhelmed. After all, I'm a lot younger than she is. Even before this happened, I thought she needed help, and now she agrees."

"The only reason *you're* exhausted is because you aren't used to doing any kind of physical work."

Sabrina told herself to be patient. "Maybe not, but I work out five days a week. I'm fit and I'm strong."

"I don't see why you can't just stay here with me until my cast comes off." Her tone said Sabrina was selfish. Furthermore, it suggested, if Sabrina really loved Isabel, she wouldn't think of not doing so.

"Mother, please. I have a full-time job. One you think is important, too. *And until now, I even had a life.* As much as I love you, I can't do this. I'll be happy to come several evenings a week and I can run errands and do other things for you, but I can't stay here. As it is, I'm neglecting my responsibilities at the paper."

"Well, I don't want a stranger in the house." Isabel's eyes had filled with tears.

Sabrina felt like crying too. Earlier she'd said Florence would be overwhelmed. Right now Sabrina felt overwhelmed herself.

"We're getting nowhere," she said wearily. "I just want you to think about this overnight, and we'll talk about it again tomorrow."

"I won't change my mind," her mother said stubbornly.

"Please, Mom. Just remember, the bottom line is, Florence can't handle everything on her own anymore, and I can't be here all the time. If you refuse to have someone here to help, you're risking Florence quitting. And if that happens, you'll really be in a fix. That's not what you want, is it?"

"Florence won't quit. She couldn't get another job as good as this one."

Sabrina wanted to scream. Sometimes her mother was so unreasonable she felt like strangling her.

"Don't be too sure. She's hinted that she wouldn't mind moving to Tucson to be close to her sister and her family, and with her experience, she could get a job easily." What Sabrina didn't say was that Florence could probably manage by working part-time, with the cash bequest Sabrina's father had left her.

When her mother didn't answer, Sabrina decided that no matter what her mother said, she was going to place an ad in the paper. And if her mother continued to make a fuss, Sabrina would enlist Leland's help. If anyone could persuade her to see reason, he could.

Thank God for Leland. Since his separation from his wife—which had now progressed to divorce proceedings—he had been a godsend. He came to see

Isabel several times a week, taking her out to dinner, taking her to the symphony in Cleveland, or just sitting and visiting with her in the evening. He was good with her and didn't seem to mind her limitations.

The only positive thing about all the turmoil surrounding her mother's fall was that it took Sabrina's mind off Gregg. But on Christmas Eve, as she helped her mother dress for the candlelight service at their church, she could no longer escape her lingering sadness and feelings of hopelessness she had felt since Gregg had suggested they needed to take a break from each other.

She wondered where he was now. She knew the restaurant was closed tonight and tomorrow. He was probably at Glynnis's, helping her get ready for Christmas day. She could picture them in Glynnis's cozy living room where a fat tree probably sat in front of the bay window. The tree wouldn't be a decorator's masterpiece as Sabrina's mother's was; instead it would have a mishmash of ornaments, some of them made by the children, with multicolored lights and garlands of popcorn or construction paper.

Christmas carols would be playing on the CD player, and Gregg and Glynnis would be sipping eggnog or wine. Later, when the children were asleep, Gregg would help put together the toys Glynnis had purchased for them.

The images were so vivid Sabrina's heart ached.

Gregg, I love you so much. Please don't give up on me completely.

"We're going to be late if we don't leave soon," her mother said.

Sabrina nodded. "I just have to brush my teeth and put on my lipstick, then I'll be ready."

When Sabrina came out of the bathroom, her mother was smoothing back her blond hair, which Sabrina had fashioned into a chignon. With only one usable arm, her mother couldn't put on her makeup or fix her hair.

"I wish I could've worn the green velvet," she said, looking with disfavor on her dark blue wool dress.

Sabrina sighed. "I know, but the sleeves couldn't accommodate your cast. But that dress looks beautiful on you, Mom, especially with your sapphires."

The sapphire bracelet and earrings were gorgeous antique pieces that had belonged to Sabrina's Grandmother Rockwell and would one day be Sabrina's.

Ignoring Sabrina's compliment, her mother glared at the offending cast. "I still can't believe I fell."

By now they were in the hallway and Sabrina opened the elevator door so her mother could ride in. Thank God the wheelchair was motorized, easy to navigate at the touch of a button or they'd *really* be in trouble Sabrina thought, imagining having to push her mother everywhere, since without the use of her right arm she'd hardly be able to propel herself.

It took another ten minutes to get her mother into her mink coat, scarf, a glove for her left hand and her mink muff for her right, then to help her maneuver the chair onto the lift for the van. Normally, when they went to church together, they took Ben's Lincoln. Now if Isabel was to go anywhere, they needed the lift since she couldn't put any weight on her arm.

The candlelight service was beautiful, but Sabrina could not banish the sadness that haunted her. Was this what her life would be like from now on? she wondered. Forever tied to Rockwell and her mother, who would grow increasingly dependent with every year?

Even if Isabel should someday accept Gregg as a part of Sabrina's life, how could Sabrina ask him to give up his restaurant and move to Rockwell? She couldn't. But she couldn't leave, either.

I need a miracle, she thought in despair.

Because as much as she wanted and needed to believe their relationship was not doomed, she was terribly afraid that it was.

Gregg and Glynnis had just finished getting the children's toys ready for the morning and were relaxing with a glass of wine and some of Glynnis's cheese sticks before turning in for the night. Gregg had decided to stay over so he'd be there in the morning when the children woke up.

"I know something is bothering you, Gregg. I wish you'd tell me what it is. Maybe I can help."

Gregg glanced over at his sister. She was curled up on one end of the sofa, and he was sprawled out at the other end. "It's that obvious, huh?"

"You've been trying to pretend everything is normal, but I know you too well. Something's got you worried."

The temptation to tell Glynnis everything was strong. "I am kind of down," he finally admitted.

"Is it a problem at work?"

"No, nothing like that."

"Does it have anything to do with the girl you've been seeing?"

He smiled wryly. After refilling his wineglass, he said, "Yeah."

"If you don't want to tell me, it's okay."

"I do want to tell you. I've wanted to tell you about her for a while, but I promised I wouldn't."

She frowned. "Promised who?"

"Ah, hell. It doesn't matter anymore. Okay, I'll tell you everything."

Glynnis sipped her wine and waited.

"The woman I've been seeing is someone you know."

"Oh?"

He could see she was straining to figure out who it might be. "It's Sabrina."

Glynnis stared at him. "Sabrina."

"Yes."

"I—I don't know what to say. I'm stunned."

"You didn't suspect anything?"

"No. I never dreamed it was her. How long have you been seeing her?"

"Since the day she came to Ivy to meet you and the kids. I went to Rockwell the next week, and I've been going there ever since."

"Are you…is this *serious?*"

"Yeah, it is. We love each other. I want to marry her."

"Oh, Gregg."

"Do you disapprove?"

"No, of course not, but Gregg…does her mother know?"

"Nope. That's the problem. Sabrina's afraid to tell her mother."

"You can't blame her. I mean, in her shoes, I'd be afraid, too."

Gregg nodded glumly. He finished his wine, thought about having another glass, then decided drowning his sorrows would only give him a hangover and would solve nothing, so he put the empty glass down.

"You know, Gregg," Glynnis said softly, "nothing would please me more than to have Sabrina as my sister-in-law, and I know that if Ben were alive, he'd be happy about it, too, but do you think it's possible? I mean, do you really think Sabrina could live with being estranged from her mother? Because that's what I envision happening."

Gregg shook his head. "No."

For a few moments, they were silent. Then gently, she said, "What are you going to do?"

"I don't know."

Glynnis's eyes were filled with sympathy. "I'm sorry, Gregg."

"Quit looking at me like that. Pretty soon I'll be crying in my beer."

"You're not drinking beer." She smiled, leaning over to squeeze his arm.

"Got any suggestions for me?"

"I wish I did."

"So you think it's hopeless, too."

"Not hopeless, no, but I think it's going to be very difficult to find any kind of happy ending here. At least not without hurting someone."

Gregg heaved a sigh. "Yeah. You're right."

"So where do things stand now with you and Sabrina?"

"I told her I thought we should cool it for a while. Being together is too hard on both of us. And the more we're together, the harder it gets."

"Does she agree?"

"She'd like to pretend the rest of the world doesn't exist. Bury our heads in the sand. She doesn't want to face reality. But I can't do that anymore. I want us to have a real relationship, one where we don't have to sneak around and lie to people." He met Glynnis's gaze. "Like you said, this situation isn't going to have a neatly wrapped happy ending. Eventually, Sabrina will have to choose. Me or her mother.'' Gregg didn't want to believe she had already chosen.

After that, there wasn't much left to say. Glynnis finished her wine, and Gregg helped her carry the dirty glasses and plates out to the kitchen. While she washed them and put them in the drainer, he turned off the outside lights and the tree lights, then locked up.

Before going to bed, she hugged him. ''I know I should mind my own business, but I have to say this. Call her tomorrow, Gregg. Don't let Christmas go by without telling her you love her. If you do, you'll be sorry.''

''Merry Christmas, Isabel.'' Leland bent down, kissed her cheek and handed her a jeweler's box wrapped with silver paper and ribbon. Then he turned to Sabrina. ''Merry Christmas, my dear.'' He kissed her cheek, too, and handed her a slightly smaller box wrapped in red foil paper with red ribbon.

Sabrina had never been so glad to see anyone. At least with Leland there, Christmas day might be cheerier than last night.

''You both look lovely today,'' he said, giving them an admiring glance. Both wore long skirts—Sabrina's red-and-green taffeta paired with a white satin blouse, and her mother's black velvet paired with a short-sleeved gray silk sweater shot through with silver threads.

Sabrina led the way into the living room where she fixed drinks for everyone, then passed a serving plate with crab puffs and mini quiches. For a few moments, they sat quietly eating and drinking and admiring the tree.

The giant spruce in front of the window had been lit earlier. It looked gorgeous, all white and gold, decorated with expensive ornaments handpicked by her mother. A local handyman had put it up for them and, under her mother's supervision, Florence and Sabrina had decorated it.

"The tree looks beautiful," Leland said.

"Thank you," Isabel said.

"But not as beautiful as the two of you."

"Oh, Leland," Isabel said.

Sabrina was amazed. If she hadn't known better, she would have said her mother was blushing.

Leland smiled. "Shall we open our gifts?"

Earlier Sabrina had removed two packages from under the tree and presented them to Leland.

"You first," Leland said to Sabrina's mother.

"Oh," she said when she lifted out a gold compact encrusted with diamonds in a heart-shaped pattern. "It's simply gorgeous. Thank you, Leland."

Sabrina stared. If she was any judge at all, that compact had cost him a fortune.

He smiled and turned to Sabrina. "Now you, my dear."

Sabrina carefully removed the ribbon and paper from her gift and opened the box. She gasped. Inside lay a delicate bangle bracelet of brushed white gold studded with tiny diamonds. She was stunned. "I—I don't know what to say," she finally murmured. "This is incredible. Thank you."

Leland beamed, obviously pleased with their reactions.

Then he opened his gifts. Sabrina's mother had given him a beautiful pair of leather gloves, and Sabrina's gift was a cashmere scarf in a soft heather blue. He seemed touched and thanked them far more profusely than the gifts warranted. Sabrina decided he was just lonely and had adopted them as his substitute family. She wondered what his children were doing for the holidays. She knew his son lived in Los Angeles and his daughter and her family lived in Connecticut.

"I have some good news for the both of you," Leland said once they were again settled with their drinks. "We have another offer, this time in writing, for Ben's company. Marcus Greenlee had it sent to my office by messenger yesterday morning."

"What kind of offer?" Sabrina's mother asked.

"It's excellent. You'll get two dollars more per share than the Kenyon people wanted to give you."

Sabrina knew her mother was adding up the amount in her head. Her smile said she was pleased.

"What kind of terms?" she asked.

While Leland was explaining the terms of the contract, Sabrina went out to the kitchen to check on the standing rib roast. Earlier she'd fixed au gratin potatoes, baked butternut squash, and a salad of romaine lettuce, toasted almonds and mandarin oranges, which she'd toss with a poppy-seed dressing right before dinner.

She had just finished giving everything a final check when her cell phone, which she'd put on the kitchen counter earlier, rang.

Sabrina grabbed it. Her heart leaped when she saw Gregg's cell phone number in the caller ID display.

"Merry Christmas," he said when she answered.

"Merry Christmas."

"I couldn't let the day go by without calling you."

Tears filled Sabrina's eyes.

"I love you, Sabrina. You know that, don't you?"

"Yes," she whispered. "And I love you."

"What are you doing now?"

She told him that Leland was there and that they would soon have dinner. "Mother seems happy today."

"Good. What about you? Are you happy?"

"I am now. Oh, Gregg, I've been so miserable since you left."

"I know. Me, too. I miss you."

"And I miss you."

They were both silent for a few seconds. Then he said, "Last night I told Glynnis about us."

"You did? What did she say?"

"She said nothing would make her happier than to have you as her sister-in-law."

"I feel the same way about her." She knuckled

away her tears. "Did the children like the gifts I sent them?"

"They loved them. Olivia squealed when she saw the doll. And Michael was so excited over the rocket ship he wanted to go outside this morning to try it out."

Sabrina smiled. Oh, she wished she could have seen their faces.

"I wish we were together today," he said.

"Me, too." She held her breath. Was he going to say he'd changed his mind? That he couldn't stay away? That he would come to see her this week?

But all he said was, "We'll talk again soon."

"Who were you talking to, dear?" Isabel asked when Sabrina rejoined her and Leland.

"Oh, just a friend who called to wish me a Merry Christmas."

Her mother studied her thoughtfully. "Is this friend that young man you mentioned?"

"What young man?"

Her mother smiled. "She's playing dumb, Leland. All right, Sabrina, have it your way. If you don't want to talk about him, we won't. I was just telling Leland before you came back that I think we should take this offer. Do you agree?"

"Whatever you want, Mom, is fine with me."

"In that case, Leland, tell them we accept."

For the rest of the day, Isabel was upbeat and talkative, and Sabrina did her best to be cheerful, too, but her heart wasn't in it. Her heart was in Ivy and there it would always remain.

The help-wanted ad Sabrina placed in the newspaper began to run the day after Christmas. The following evening, she received a call from Emma Phillips, the mother of a girl she'd gone to high school with.

"So you remember me, Sabrina?"

"Mrs. Phillips! Of course I remember you. How are you?"

"I'm doing okay. It's hard without Jonah, but I'm managing."

Belatedly, Sabrina remembered that Emma Phillips's husband had died of cancer the previous year. "I'm sorry about Mr. Phillips."

"Thank you. Sabrina, the reason I called is I saw your ad for a nurse's aide. My sister Elaine is living with me now and she's a nurse. I know you said an aide, but Elaine is really good with handicapped people. In Syracuse, where she lived until her divorce, she worked at a rehabilitation center, so she's used to handling people in wheelchairs."

"I'm not sure this will be a permanent position."

"She knows that. She likes the idea of a temporary job right now. That'll give her time to figure out what she wants to do on a more permanent basis. And if your mother should decide she likes Elaine and wants to keep her on, well, then they can discuss it when the time comes."

Sabrina liked Elaine Macy immediately. An attractive, no-nonsense type with short dark hair and a face filled with laugh lines, the nurse seemed knowledgeable, capable and not easily rattled.

"I'll warn you right now," Sabrina said, "my mother can be difficult."

Elaine Macy smiled. "I'm used to difficult patients. Thing is, most of them have it rough. I just try to make life easier for them, and they usually come around."

So Sabrina hired her. Then she faced the job of telling her mother what she'd done.

To Sabrina's astonishment, Isabel didn't put up a fight. "Leland said you were right," she admitted. "He said I was being stubborn."

Since Leland had performed *this* miracle, Sabrina wondered if he might be able to perform another, this time about her relationship with Gregg. She vowed then and there that once the sale of the company had gone through and the closing was over, she would find the courage to talk to her mother, and if necessary, she'd ask Leland for his help.

Sabrina couldn't wait for the closing, which was to take place in mid January.

Things had settled down at the house since Elaine had started working there, and Sabrina was now back in her apartment.

She and Gregg talked by phone every few days,

and she'd told him of her decision to tell her mother about him as soon as the closing was over.

They still weren't seeing each other, but Sabrina was finally hopeful that a solution to their problem would be found, because she simply couldn't stand the alternative.

Finally the day of the closing arrived. About ten that morning, Vicki buzzed Sabrina to say Leland Fox was on the line for her.

"Good morning, Leland," Sabrina said. She lifted her arm to let the white gold bracelet he'd given her catch the light. "I'm wearing your bracelet today. Thank you again. I really love it."

"You're very welcome. Listen, Sabrina, something completely unexpected has happened. Something that is going to upset your mother very much, I'm afraid."

Sabrina's heart sank. What now? "What is it?" she asked.

"You know I called the brokerage house in Cleveland to tell them to send me all the shares they were holding."

"Yes."

"Well, they came this morning. Sabrina, it looks like several weeks before his death, your father signed over the bulk of the shares that were in his name to the two children he had with Glynnis."

Sabrina was speechless.

"I had no idea he'd done this. All that's left in his

name is twelve percent of the total shares. You know what this means, don't you?''

''It…it means my mother and I will only receive payment for the twenty-four percent we each own outright and we'll split the twelve percent.''

''Yes, you'll each end up with thirty percent of the total and your father's two younger children will get eleven percent each.''

This revelation was almost too enormous to absorb. Sabrina certainly didn't care that Glynnis's children now owned some of the stock—in fact, she was happy for them and for Glynnis—but she knew her mother would go crazy.

''What are we going to do about the closing? Can we postpone it for a while? At least until we've had a chance to talk to Mother?''

''I'll call Marcus Greenlee, but I don't think he'll be happy. My recommendation would be to go ahead with the closing and worry about the stock later, when the money for the company is in hand.''

''I don't know if Mother will agree to that.''

''Let me call Marcus and see what he says. I'll call you back.''

Ten minutes later Leland was on the line again. ''He says he'll wait one more week, but that's it. If we don't close next Tuesday, the deal's off.''

''I guess I'd better go and see Mother right away. Will you come with me?''

''Of course. Can you leave right now?''

''Yes.''

"Then I'll meet you there in twenty minutes."

Sabrina couldn't help but remember the last time Leland had met her outside her mother's to help her deliver bad news. She hoped Isabel would take this news better than she'd taken the former.

Her hopes were futile.

Her mother was livid when Leland told her about the transferred stock. "There is no way I will allow twenty-two percent of our company to go to those children," she said tightly.

"But Mother," Sabrina said, "it's not our choice. They own the stock."

"Not for long. I'll contest this. I'll take them to court."

"On what grounds?" Leland asked.

"That Ben wasn't in his right mind when he signed that stock over to them. They have no legal right to those shares. None at all."

Leland tried talking to her, to no avail. He then called Bob Culberson, who also tried talking to Isabel. He told her the offer was the best they could ever hope to get. Leland said that even without the twenty-two percent now owned by Glynnis's children, she and Sabrina would still receive substantial sums. He also told her she didn't have a good case and that she could end up spending a lot of money going to court, and end up with nothing more than she had now.

But Isabel was adamant. "How do I even know those children are Ben's?" she demanded.

"Mother, please don't do this," Sabrina pleaded. She couldn't imagine what a lawsuit would do to Glynnis.

And Gregg. Dear Lord, he would be furious on his sister's behalf, and Sabrina wouldn't blame him.

What would he say?

She dreaded calling him, but she couldn't put it off. She waited until she knew the lunch business would have cleared out, then she put in a call to him.

"Hi," he said. "Is the closing over already?"

"It was canceled."

"Canceled? You mean they backed out?"

"No. Something else happened. That's why I'm calling. To tell you about it." She explained about Leland asking the brokerage house to send over the stock. "I don't know if I told you about the stock or not, but my mother and I both own a certain percentage of my father's company shares outright. Our general manager also owns some of the shares. The rest—thirty-four percent of the total—were in my father's name. According to his will, any shares he owned at the time of his death were to be divided between me and my mother equally. Today we learned that my father no longer owns most of those shares. A few weeks before he died, he transferred the bulk of the shares to Michael and Olivia."

"How much are we talking about here?"

"Based on the Greenlee offer of four million dollars, the twenty-two percent of the company that the children now own is worth eight hundred and eighty thousand dollars.''

Gregg whistled. "How do you feel about this?''

"I think it's wonderful, but my mother is extremely upset. In fact…'' Here Sabrina took a deep breath. "She says she's going to contest the transfer of stock in court.''

"On what basis?''

"She says my father wasn't in his right mind when he did this. She…'' Sabrina swallowed. "She's even questioning the children's parentage.''

"What?''

"I'm sorry. I—''

"You being sorry isn't going to do Glynnis or those kids a helluva lot of good, is it?''

"Don't yell at *me,* Gregg. I haven't done anything.''

"I'm sorry,'' he said more quietly, "I know this isn't your fault. I'm just so damned mad! I can't believe your mother wants to drag this mess into the courts. Can't you talk some sense into her?''

"No one can tell my mother anything.''

"Well, if she thinks she's going to scare Glynnis off with these tactics, she's got another think coming. My sister isn't to blame for any of this. Your father is. And as far as I'm concerned, he owes Glynnis and those kids. I'm glad to see he finally realized that. So if your mother wants a court fight, then by God, she'll get one.''

His reaction was even worse than Sabrina had imagined it would be.

A few moments later, he said he had to go, that he'd talk to her later, after he'd had a chance to talk to Glynnis. But Sabrina knew if and when they did talk again, nothing would change. Any slim hope she might have still been holding out for a future with Gregg was now permanently gone.

Chapter Eleven

Gregg put his head in his hands and groaned. Why had he yelled at Sabrina? She was right. None of this was her fault. But dammit! The thought of having Glynnis and those kids dragged through the mud because Sabrina's mother refused to concede that Ben March had done the right thing by acknowledging that he owed them something infuriated him.

There was no way Gregg was going to sit idly by and let her get away with this.

Telling first Mark and then Janine that he had something to take care of and would be gone for at least an hour, he headed for the college. He was halfway there when he realized he should have called Glynnis first. Whipping out his cell phone, he punched in the code for her office. When he heard her voice, he said, "Oh good, you're there. I'm on my way over. I need to talk to you."

"Gregg, is something wrong?"

"No, it's just that something has happened, and I need to tell you about it."

"I've got a class in ten minutes."

"Can you get someone to cover for you?"

"That won't be easy, but I guess I could try."

"Well, try. If not, I'll wait till your class is over."

"It's a two-hour class."

"Ah, hell. I should have called you before I left, I guess."

"Let me see what I can do. You're on your cell, right? I'll call you right back."

Gregg was already pulling into the college parking lot when his phone rang.

"Judith said she'd cover the class for the first hour."

"Come on out then. I'm in the front parking lot. We'll go get coffee somewhere."

A few minutes later, Glynnis emerged looking more like one of the kids she taught than a teacher. In jeans, high-heeled boots and a dark green parka, she looked at least ten years younger than she was. Her bright hair blew around her face. He leaned over and opened the passenger door for her.

She smiled. "Hi." Her eyes were curious, but she didn't question him and he didn't volunteer anything until they were seated across from each other at a small table in a neighboring Starbucks.

"I've got some news," he said. "Both good and not so good."

She sipped at her latte and waited.

"I think I mentioned that one of the big tour companies had made an offer to buy Ben's company."

"Yes."

"The closing was supposed to take place today."

"And?"

"And it didn't, because some new information came to light. That's the good news."

"I don't understand."

"A few weeks before Ben died, he signed over twenty-two percent of the company stock, which is worth close to nine hundred thousand dollars, to the kids. To Michael and Olivia."

Glynnis stared at him.

"This was stock that Sabrina and her mother believed belonged to them," Gregg added.

Glynnis put her latte down. She looked stunned.

"The bad news is," Gregg continued, "that Sabrina's mother is furious about this and is threatening to contest ownership of the stock in court. According to Sabrina, her mother is saying that Ben wasn't in his right mind when he transferred that stock to the kids."

"This is unbelievable. I—I didn't even know Ben owned a company. That was one of the things he kept hidden, I'm sure because he was afraid I might try to reach him there, and he couldn't take that chance.''

''I know.''

She looked out the window. Two young girls, laughing and talking, passed by. Glynnis seemed unaware of them, even when they looked in the window and, giggling, waved at her. Finally she turned back to Gregg. Her eyes were troubled.

''I'm so touched that Ben did this for me and the children, but if it's going to cause problems, then I don't want the money. Tell Sabrina that as the children's guardian, I'll give the stock back to her and her mother.''

''You absolutely will not! Those kids have as much right to a share in their father's company as Sabrina or her mother.''

''But Gregg—''

''Look, Glynnis, I know you want to be fair, but this *is* fair. I happen to know that Sabrina and her mother each already own twenty-four percent of the company stock, plus they'll be getting another six percent each from Ben. That means they'll end up with more than a million bucks apiece out of this sale. Why shouldn't Michael and Olivia have a share? They're his kids, too, and that money will insure their future, enable them to go to the best schools, and give all of you some security. I'm sure Ben was thinking about that when he signed the stock over to them. I don't think you have the right to go against his wishes or to give away their inheritance.''

''I just hate causing any more pain to Sabrina's mother. She's already had to bear so much.''

''You know, I'm sick of hearing about Sabrina's mother.''

''Gregg.''

For a moment, Gregg was ashamed of himself. But dammit, he *was* sick of hearing about Sabrina's mother. Glynnis had been through a lot, too, but she wasn't feeling sorry for herself. ''Look, you've got to put the welfare of your kids first. Let Sabrina worry about her mother.''

''That money *would* make our lives so much easier.''

''Yes, it would.''

Glynnis sighed. ''Okay. You've convinced me. We won't give it up voluntarily. But oh, God, Gregg, I hate the idea of a court battle.''

Gregg figured he might as well tell her all of it. ''It's gonna get ugly. Sabrina's mother is even questioning whether or not the kids are Ben's.''

''*What?*''

''That's what Sabrina told me.''

''You don't think anyone will believe that, do you?''

''Doesn't matter what they believe. Ben acknowledged them as his. That's what counts.''

She nodded, but she didn't seem convinced.

Reaching across the table, he grasped her hand.

"Glynnie, don't worry. You don't have to do this alone. I'll be with you all the way."

"I know. Thank God for you. I—I don't think I could face this by myself."

Gregg put his arm around her as they walked out of the shop. He knew the upcoming proceedings were probably a death sentence for him and Sabrina, and a part of him mourned, but the other part of him, the part that had always vowed to look out for his twin after their parents died, was more determined than ever.

If Isabel March wanted a fight, by damn, she was going to get one.

The closing took place a week later than originally scheduled. Because ownership of a percentage of the shares in the company were in dispute, that portion of the money from the sale was put into an escrow account. Depending upon the outcome of Isabel's suit, it would be distributed to the appropriate parties.

Sabrina's mother was convinced she would win in court, a belief strengthened when she was told Judge Hannah Winslow would preside.

"Why, Hannah and I have known each other for years," she crowed. "We were in the same sorority."

Sabrina didn't comment. Anything she said that wasn't in agreement with her mother would only cause trouble between them, and what would be the point of that?

"Hannah's known to be tough but fair," Leland said in a cautionary tone.

"Then I have nothing to worry about," Isabel said. "Because I'm in the right."

The day of the trial dawned cold and gray, just like Sabrina's mood. She dreaded going to court, dreaded seeing Gregg and Glynnis, dreaded the whole miserable process.

She had only talked to Gregg once during the past weeks, and that conversation was totally unsatisfactory, reinforcing her belief that any hope for a relationship between them was finished.

Thinking back over the conversation, she thought maybe she shouldn't have asked him to pretend he didn't know her when he saw her in court, but how could she not? Her mother had no idea she'd met Gregg and Glynnis. Sabrina had to ask him not to acknowledge her. To do otherwise would have been stupid and only thrown more fuel on the fire of her mother's wrath.

But Gregg had chosen to view her request as another indication that her mother was more important to her than he was. When she'd tried to explain that she didn't want her mother to become even more vindictive toward Glynnis than she already was and that if she felt Sabrina had any kind of sympathetic feelings toward him or his sister, that's exactly what would happen, he'd brushed aside her explanation.

"Don't worry about it," he'd said. "You're safe."

"It's not *me* I'm worried about!" she'd cried.

Their goodbye had been awkward, with no mention of talking again, and—most significantly—without exchanging any loving words. Sabrina wanted to say "I love you" but she felt too raw and too afraid. What if he answered back by saying he no longer loved *her?*

"Why are you so gloomy today, Sabrina?" her mother asked as they entered the courthouse. "Trust me. This is going to work out very well for us."

Sabrina couldn't answer. No matter what the outcome today, it wouldn't be good news for Sabrina.

"Oh, there's Leland," her mother said.

Sabrina turned to see Leland striding toward them. As always, he was dressed impeccably—today in a charcoal suit, white shirt and striped tie. He smiled as he approached. "Good morning. How are you two doing today?"

"Wonderful," Isabel said.

"We're fine," Sabrina said. Why on earth was her mother so cheerful? It was almost as if she was relishing the upcoming fight.

Sabrina looked around, half hoping to see Gregg and half afraid she would.

"Let's go," Leland said, "we're in Courtroom Number Four, upstairs. The elevators are around the corner."

Sabrina took a deep breath as they entered the courtroom, a breath she slowly let out in relief when she realized neither Gregg nor Glynnis had yet arrived. Leland led them to the front of the room and indicated that they should be seated behind the table to the left of the judge's bench. "Plaintiffs always sit on this side of the court," he explained.

Sabrina checked her watch. It was ten minutes before ten, and the trial was scheduled to begin at ten. Her stomach was filled with butterflies as she anticipated the arrival of Gregg and Glynnis, which would probably take place at any moment. Sure enough, less than a minute later, the two of them, accompanied by their lawyer—a smart-looking young woman in a black, pinstriped suit—walked in.

Glynnis looked beautiful in a wool dress the shade of nutmeg under a camel-colored coat. And Gregg... Sabrina's heart beat faster just looking at him. Love nearly overwhelmed her as her eyes drank him in. For the briefest moment, his gaze met hers, then he deliberately looked away. Her heart beat painfully in her chest. Why did love have to hurt so much?

Turning away, she saw that her mother was staring at Glynnis. Sabrina couldn't imagine how her mother must feel. It must hurt unbearably to come face-to-face with the younger woman, to know that her husband had wanted her enough to commit bigamy and that she had given him two children—children Isabel couldn't have.

"All rise," the bailiff said. "The Honorable Hannah Winslow presiding."

The judge came in through a door behind the bench and took her seat. As soon as she was seated, everyone else sat down again. Sabrina recognized the judge. In her earlier days at the paper, she'd covered several trials where Judge Winslow had presided.

For the next twenty minutes, the opposing lawyers presented various documents to be admitted into evidence. One was an affidavit signed by an officer at the brokerage house saying he'd witnessed Sabrina's father signing away the disputed shares. Copies of the shares in question were also presented. Copies of the birth certificates of Michael and Olivia were introduced, as was a copy of the marriage certificate of Glynnis and Sabrina's father.

When Glynnis's lawyer introduced these documents, Sabrina glanced at her mother to see how she was bearing up. Her mother's lips tightened, but otherwise her cool demeanor didn't change.

Leland, however, immediately objected.

"Your Honor," he said, "my client, Isabel Rockwell March, is the legal spouse of Benjamin Arthur March, who passed away last October. His subsequent marriage to Glynnis Antonelli is not recognized by the state as it is a bigamous relationship. Therefore, these documents have no bearing on this proceeding."

"Your Honor," Glynnis's lawyer—whose name was Diane Clemmons—said, "these documents have *everything* to do with this proceeding. They are, in fact, the basis of my entire argument for my client. She did not know Benjamin March was already married when she entered into her marriage with him, and he freely acknowledged his parentage of her children. He was present at their births, and he allowed his name to be entered as their father. For purposes of his intent, these documents must be entered into the record.''

"Whether she knew Mr. March's marital status is a moot point, Your Honor,'' Leland countered. ''And Mr. March's name is not the one entered as their father. Their father is listed as Benjamin Arthur.''

"Mr. Fox is splitting hairs, Your Honor,'' Diane Clemmons said. ''We all know Mr. March used the name Arthur to hide the fact he was already married.''

"That's what you *say,*'' Leland began. ''However—''

Judge Winslow held up her hand. ''Enough. The documents in question can be entered into the record.'' When Leland started to protest, she turned to him. ''Mr. Fox, I concur that the marriage itself is not relevant, but the birth of the children *is,* and although you would like us to have doubts as to their father's identity, I think we all know that Benjamin March is the Benjamin Arthur in question. Therefore the documents are admissible. Shall we proceed?''

The last document to be entered into evidence was the marriage certificate of Sabrina's parents, to which there were no objections.

Then it was time for the lawyers to present their respective cases. As the lawyer for the plaintiff, Leland would go first.

"Your Honor," he said, "I would like to call my first witness, Isabel Rockwell March."

Sabrina watched as her mother was sworn in. Since she still had a cast on her right arm, she raised her left to take her oath. Throughout, she never turned her eyes in the direction of Glynnis.

"Mrs. March," Leland said, "you married Benjamin March thirty-one years ago, is that correct?"

"Yes, it is."

"And your daughter, Sabrina, was born three years later."

"Yes, that's correct." Isabel's gray gaze, so like Sabrina's, rested on Sabrina's face for a few moments before turning back to Leland.

"When you married your husband, did he have a job?"

"Yes, he did. He worked for a large, national travel agency. He organized special tours for them."

"When did he start March Tours?"

"After our daughter was born, he asked me if I'd be willing to lend him the money to open his own tour company. He had prepared a lengthy business plan and done a great deal of research and felt there was a niche for a high-end company."

"And did you agree?"

"After doing some research of my own, yes."

"So you lent him the money?"

"Yes."

"Just so the court will understand, this was money

you had inherited from your grandparents before your marriage to your husband, isn't that right?''

"Yes."

"And in return for lending your husband the money, what did you receive?"

"He signed a note agreeing to pay me back within ten years, and he also agreed that Sabrina and I would each own twenty percent of the company."

"And did he pay you back in ten years?"

"Yes, he did."

Sabrina wondered what Gregg was thinking as they listened to her mother testify. Even though Sabrina wished she were anywhere else but there, and even though she thought her mother's actions were misguided, she couldn't help being proud of the way Isabel conducted herself. She was calm and in control and gave her answers quietly and without theatrics.

Leland continued, "According to documentation introduced to the court this morning, at the time of your husband's death, you and your daughter each owned twenty-four percent of the company, not twenty percent."

"Yes, that's right. Three years ago, at Christmas, Ben presented each of us with four percent more."

"Mrs. March, please tell the court why you believe your husband was not in possession of his full faculties when he signed over twenty-two percent of the company to the children of Ms. Antonelli."

"Objection, Your Honor," Miss Clemmons said.

"Mrs. March is not a doctor, therefore her opinion as to the mental faculties of Benjamin March has no merit whatsoever."

"On the contrary, Your Honor," Leland countered, "by virtue of the length of Mrs. March's marriage to Benjamin March, she is the only person in this courtroom—indeed, in this *world*—who is qualified to speak about Mr. March's mental state during the month before his death."

"Your Honor," Miss Clemmons said, "this is ridiculous. If the plaintiff is correct about Mr. March's mental faculties, then she should be able to back up her contention with expert testimony from Mr. March's doctor."

Judge Winslow spoke before Leland could counter, saying, "I will bear in mind that whatever Mrs. March says is simply her opinion. I'll allow the question."

Diane Clemmons looked as if she'd like to say something else, but she refrained.

"Go ahead, Mrs. March," Leland said. "Tell the court why you believe your husband wasn't in possession of his full faculties when he signed over those shares to Ms. Antonelli's children."

"It's obvious, isn't it? He was brainwashed into thinking those children were fathered by him, but I don't believe they were."

"Oh, *please,* Your Honor," Miss Clemmons said, jumping up. "This is totally ridiculous."

"Sit down, Miss Clemmons. You've already made

your objections known. The witness can finish testifying.''

''Why do you believe Ms. Antonelli's children weren't fathered by your husband?'' Leland asked.

''Because for years after Sabrina was born we tried to have more children, with no success. When she was six, we were both tested. My tests showed there was nothing wrong with me, but Ben's tests showed his sperm count was too low, and that's why I hadn't gotten pregnant again.''

Sabrina stared at her mother. Was this true? It must be, or Leland would never have allowed her to say it. Besides, her mother might have many faults, but she was not a liar. In fact, Sabrina had never known her mother to tell a lie, not even a white one. She always said people who lied were stupid, because they always got caught.

But Sabrina had seen those children. It was true that Olivia looked like her mother, but no one who knew Sabrina's father could look at Michael and not know his parentage. He was the image of her father.

Sabrina couldn't stop herself from looking in Glynnis's and Gregg's direction. They had their heads together, talking quietly. Neither noticed her watching them. Sabrina's heart ached. She knew Glynnis would never have cheated on her father. Those two kids were her father's. There was no doubt in her mind.

Could her father have fudged the truth with her mother? Maybe he hadn't wanted her to be hurt.

Maybe there had been nothing at all wrong with his sperm count, and he had just told her that so that she wouldn't realize it was *her* fault they couldn't have another child.

Sabrina realized speculation was futile. The only person who could shed any light on what her mother had just said was dead. They would never know the truth.

"Thank you, Mrs. March. That's all for now," Leland said. He smiled at Sabrina's mother, his expression saying she'd done a good job.

"Do you wish to question the witness, Miss Clemmons?" the judge asked.

"Yes, I certainly do, Your Honor." Diane Clemmons rose. She walked purposefully toward Isabel. Her tone was challenging. "Mrs. March, all we have is your word for what allegedly happened when those supposed tests were made. If what you said is true, where's the paperwork? Where's the proof?"

Sabrina bit her lip, but her mother wasn't the least bit rattled by the attorney's question or her aggressive manner.

"Those tests were conducted twenty-two years ago, Miss Clemmons. The doctor who administered them has been dead for more than a dozen years. None of his records are still available."

"Excuse me? Do you mean to tell me you and your husband didn't obtain your medical records when you found a new physician? I assume you *did* find a new doctor?"

"Yes, of course, we did. But the records were incomplete." Isabel sighed. "Apparently Dr. Waddell's office staff wasn't as thorough as they should have been." Suddenly Isabel turned to the judge. "Hannah, this can all be—"

Judge Winslow gave Sabrina's mother a stern look. "Mrs. March, you will please address me as Your Honor or Judge Winslow."

"I'm sorry, Your Honor. What I was going to say was, whether there are records of our tests or not isn't relevant. This can all be settled by a paternity test. DNA can be obtained from my husband and it can be compared to the DNA of those two children. I'm confident testing will prove indisputably that he did not father them."

Sabrina looked at Gregg. But he wasn't looking her way. Instead, he beckoned Glynnis's lawyer to the table.

"I'd like a word with my client, Your Honor," she said.

"Keep it brief, please," the judge said.

Glynnis's lawyer walked over to where she and Gregg were sitting, and the three of them conferred for a few moments. Then Glynnis's lawyer walked back to the bench. "Your Honor, my client has no objection to a paternity test, on one condition."

"And that is?"

"That Sabrina March should also be tested."

"What?" Isabel said. "That's ridiculous! How

dare you!'' For only the second time that day, she looked directly at Glynnis.

''That's enough, Mrs. March,'' the judge said. ''I will decide what is and isn't ridiculous. Actually, I think the request is a fair one. If any of the children are to be tested, they should all be tested.''

Ignoring the renewed protests of both Leland and Isabel, she continued. ''The body of Benjamin Arthur March shall be exhumed for the purpose of obtaining a DNA sample. DNA samples shall also be obtained from Sabrina March, Michael Antonelli March, and Olivia Caroline March. When the results are known, I will make my final decision regarding ownership of the disputed shares of stock in Mr. March's company.''

''Leland, do something!'' Isabel said. ''You can't let them do this. I won't allow it.''

Judge Winslow banged her gavel and gave Sabrina's mother a hard look. ''You have no choice, Mrs. March. I've made my ruling. If you refuse to follow it, I'll hold you in contempt of court.''

Chapter Twelve

Gregg and Glynnis were staying at the Rockwell Inn overnight. Gregg stood in the sitting room of their suite and looked out the window overlooking the gardens while Glynnis called home to talk to the children. Even now, at twilight, the view was beautiful. The trees surrounding the golf course were etched inky black against the violet sky, and the snow-covered ground glistened in the fading light. As he watched, a deer darted across the fairway, then disappeared in the woods beyond.

"Have you finished your homework, Michael?" Glynnis was asking. "You have? Did Steve go over your reading words with you? He did? And what did you eat for dinner? Oh, I see. Burger boy. Did you tell Steve I don't approve of fast food?'' Then she laughed. ''I know. It was a special occasion.''

Gregg remembered how Sabrina had wished he could stay at the inn those times he'd come to Rockwell to see her. Now here he was. But he might as well have been a thousand miles away for all the good it did him where she was concerned. He wondered if he would ever come to Rockwell again. After today, he didn't think much of his chances.

After talking to Olivia—a conversation that made Gregg smile because he could picture his precocious niece chattering away at the other end—Glynnis said goodbye. ''Ready?'' she said to Gregg.

He turned. ''Yeah, I'm ready.'' They were meeting Diane Clemmons downstairs in the dining room for an early dinner and to discuss the day and future strategy.

Gregg wasn't unhappy with the way things had turned out today, even though Glynnis had never gotten a chance to say a word. He knew what the results of the DNA testing would be, and he felt sure once the judge knew, she would rule in their favor.

Steve was bringing the children to Rockwell in the morning. The same doctor would take blood samples from them as well as from Sabrina. Gregg still felt a little guilty about that, because it had been his idea to demand that Sabrina also be tested. But he felt if Glynnis had to be put through this indignity, then Sabrina's mother should have to endure the same. He wondered if Sabrina minded. Her mother sure hadn't been happy about it.

Isabel March was exactly the kind of woman he'd pictured her to be: elegant, beautiful, composed and cold. An ice queen. It amazed Gregg that a woman like Isabel could have given birth to a daughter like Sabrina, for the two women were nothing alike. Their only similarity, as far as he could see, was the color of their eyes, but whereas Isabel's were frosty, Sabrina's were soft, like the morning mist.

Sabrina...

He wondered if he'd ever stop loving her.

Was there any hope for them at all?

Ben's body would be exhumed tomorrow. After that, it would only be a matter of a couple of days before the results of the testing were known.

Then who knew what would happen? Whatever it was, Gregg knew it would affect his future as much or more than it affected Glynnis's and the children's.

He and Glynnis were leaving after the children's testing tomorrow. There was no point in waiting around in Rockwell. When the results were finalized, they would be notified. If Glynnis then had to make another appearance in court, she would come back.

As they rode the elevator down to the main level of the inn, Gregg's thoughts once again turned to Sabrina.

It had been hard sitting in the same room with her today and not being able to acknowledge her. Several times, he'd sneaked a look at her. She'd seemed so distant. What they'd been to each other seemed like something he'd imagined, and that hurt.

Remembering, the hurt returned.

"You're thinking about Sabrina, aren't you?" Glynnis said as they exited the elevator. She slipped her arm through his and gave him an understanding smile.

"Yeah."

"Today was rough."

"Yeah."

"I'm so sorry, Gregg. You know that, don't you?"

He smiled wryly. "Yeah, I know that."

"I love her, too."

"I know you do."

Glynnis sighed. "Today, during the proceedings, watching her mother, I thought about all the pain Ben had caused. You know, up until now, I've defended him, but what he did was very wrong. He should never have lied to me in the first place. I still can't be sorry about our relationship, because I wouldn't trade Michael and Olivia for anything in the world, but I do hate how many people he hurt in the process."

Gregg had gotten over his hatred of Ben. Actually, now he felt sorry for him. As Glynnis had said when she'd first learned of his duplicity, he must have felt desperate to do what he had.

By now they'd entered the dining room, and Gregg spied Diane Clemmons sitting at a window table. She stood when she saw them and waved. He noticed that she'd changed out of her businesslike suit into a short black dress that showed off rather spectacular legs.

"Maybe I should have changed into something else," Glynnis said.

"You look great."

"She looks better."

Gregg grinned.

Diane greeted them both warmly, and if her hand lingered in Gregg's a few seconds longer than necessary, it might have been accidental.

"I think things went very well today," she said when they were seated. "And since I'm sure the DNA testing will be favorable, I think we're going to win this." She smiled at Glynnis, then turned to Gregg. Her green eyes were speculative as they met his. "Do you plan to wait here until the results are in?"

Gregg shook his head. "We're going home tomorrow. Whether we stay here or not isn't going to make a difference to the outcome."

"That's too bad. I was looking forward to getting to know you better." She turned to Glynnis. "Both of you."

Gregg knew when a woman was coming on to him, and Diane Clemmons definitely was. In another lifetime, he might have been interested. She was a beautiful woman. Unfortunately, since meeting Sabrina, no other woman held any appeal.

"Did Gregg tell you he owns a restaurant?" Glynnis said.

Diane raised her eyebrows. "Really? What kind?"

Gregg was in the middle of telling her about Antonelli's when he saw Glynnis stiffen. She was looking over his shoulder. He knew even before he turned around that he would see Sabrina.

All afternoon, Sabrina had tried to calm her mother. "I don't mind being tested," she'd said, over and over again, but her mother wouldn't be calmed. Nothing Sabrina said made any difference.

Finally Leland said, "Isabel, please, let's forget about all this for a while. I'll take you both to dinner at the Rockwell Inn."

"Florence has already prepared dinner," Isabel said. But she stopped wringing her handkerchief.

"I'll tell her to put it in the refrigerator. We'll have it tomorrow," Sabrina said.

"Well..." Isabel sniffed.

Sabrina smiled for the first time in hours. She thanked Leland silently. A change of scenery was just what they all needed. And her mother loved going to the Rockwell Inn.

"I'll need to change clothes," Isabel said.

"You look fine just the way you are," Leland said.

"Leland, I cannot wear this tonight after wearing it all day."

He smiled and winked at Sabrina. "All right. But hurry. I'm starving."

"I told you to eat some lunch," Isabel said, but she was smiling, too.

Once again Sabrina marveled at how easily Leland could coax her mother out of a bad mood. Now if Sabrina could only bottle whatever it was he had, her life would be a lot easier.

Forty minutes later the three of them were led into the dining room by the hostess, a young woman Sabrina had gone to high school with. Halfway between the entrance and their table, Sabrina realized Gregg and Glynnis and their lawyer were also there. Her heart knocked painfully as Glynnis's eyes met hers.

A moment later, Gregg turned, and their gazes connected. *Oh, Gregg.* She wanted so much to walk over to their table and give Glynnis a hug and Gregg a kiss. She tried to tell him with her eyes what she was feeling. When he abruptly turned around again, putting his back to her, it was as if he'd slapped her.

She was trembling inside when the hostess seated them at a table across the room from where Gregg and Glynnis were sitting. She wondered if her mother or Leland had noticed them yet.

A moment later, her mother's expression hardened. "What are those people doing here?" she said tightly.

"What people?" Leland said. He turned to look in the direction of Isabel's gaze. "Oh." He patted her hand. "I'm sorry, Isabel. I had no idea they'd be here."

"Shall we go somewhere else?" Sabrina said.

"I will not allow those people to ruin my evening," her mother said. "It's bad enough they've ruined just about everything else."

"Now Isabel," Leland said.

"They have their nerve. Look at them, especially *her*. Has the woman no shame?"

"Mother, she didn't do anything to you. Dad's the one who's responsible for everything. She's suffered just as much as you have." As soon as the words were out of her mouth, Sabrina wished she could take them back. *When will I ever learn?*

Her mother stared at Sabrina.

"I'm sorry," Sabrina said. Oh, God. Would this day never end? She hadn't thought it could get any worse, but she was wrong.

"Just whose side are you on?" her mother said.

"I'm not on anyone's side."

"I see," her mother said tightly.

"Isabel," Leland said.

Sabrina was very close to tears. "Mom, I didn't mean it that way. I just meant I don't think of this as choosing sides. What's happened is terrible. For everyone."

"I don't see how it's terrible for *her*. She and those children of hers have come out of this very well, haven't they?" Her eyes glittered. "If there's any justice in the world at all, after today I'll never have to lay eyes on her again."

Sabrina pushed her chair back. "I—I'm not feeling well. Mother, Leland, I'm sorry, but I'm going home.'' Without waiting to hear their answers, she grabbed her purse and walked blindly out of the room.

The results of the DNA testing came back two days later. When Dr. Zeller called with the results, Sabrina had to ask him to repeat them twice, because she couldn't believe what she'd heard.

''The tests show conclusively that Michael and Olivia March are the biological children of Benjamin Arthur March. However, the tests also show conclusively that you are not his biological child.''

''But that can't be!'' Sabrina cried. ''There has to be some mistake.''

''I'm sorry, Miss March. I know this must be a terrible shock to you, but there's no mistake. Benjamin March was not your biological father.''

Sabrina hung up the phone in a daze. All the normal workday sounds surrounded her—the clicking of computer keys, the ringing of the phone, several different conversations going at one time, the hum of the copier, the jangle of the bell announcing a visitor out front—yet none of it seemed real to her. She stared into space, trying to absorb the incomprehensible information she'd just been given.

''Sabrina?''

Sabrina turned. Vicki stood in the doorway.

''You all right?''

She nodded slowly. ''Yes, I'm…I'm all right.''

''Are you *sure?*''

"Yes." But her mind was spinning. If Ben wasn't her father, who *was?* Who the hell *was?* Abruptly, Sabrina jumped up. In the process, she knocked over her coffee cup. Coffee spread over her desk, but she ignored it. "Vicki, I've got to go and do something. I don't know when I'll be back. If you need me, call my cell. And please clean up that coffee, will you? I'll owe you one."

Fifteen minutes later Sabrina braked to a stop in her mother's driveway. Her heart was pounding as she got out of the car and walked to the front door. Using her key, she unlocked it and stepped inside.

"Oh! Sabrina!" Florence, drying her hands on her apron, appeared in the entryway. "What's wrong?"

Sabrina shook her head. "Where's Mother?" ·

"She's in the sunroom." Florence looked bewildered.

Sabrina took off her coat and handed it to Florence. Then she headed for the sunroom. Her mother didn't hear her approach, so Sabrina had a chance to study her for a moment before she was aware of Sabrina's presence.

As always, her mother looked immaculate and perfectly put together. Today she wore dark gray wool slacks and a pale yellow cashmere sweater set. The pearls that had been a wedding present from her father lay around her neck. Her blond hair was worn down today and curled softly around her chin. She was watching a pair of cardinals feeding at one of the bird feeders that dotted the side yard. The male's bright red plumage was in stark contrast to the fresh snow that had fallen that morning.

Something inside Sabrina twisted painfully. Clearing her throat, she said, "Hello, Mother."

Her mother turned. "Sabrina! I didn't expect you." Her gaze met Sabrina's, and she smiled uncertainly. "What is it?"

Sabrina walked in and sat on the edge of the cushioned wicker sofa. "Dr. Zeller called me awhile ago."

Sabrina had always scoffed inwardly when she'd read about the color draining from a person's face, but that's exactly what happened then. Her mother's face went white, and her right hand—which had only yesterday had the cast removed—clasped her left hand.

Looking at the dawning fear in her mother's eyes, Sabrina understood everything. No wonder her mother had been so upset when the judge ordered DNA testing of Sabrina. She'd been afraid of exactly this outcome.

"Michael and Olivia's tests prove without a doubt that they are Dad's children," Sabrina said flatly. "But my test proves something quite different. My test proves that I was fathered by someone else."

Sabrina's mother closed her eyes. A rapid pulse beat in her throat.

"But you already knew what the tests would say, didn't you? That's why you were so against my being tested. My question now is, if Dad wasn't really my father, who is?'' Sabrina was surprised she managed to sound so calm when inside she was a chaotic mess.

Her mother opened eyes filled with tears. "Sabrina," she whispered.

"Did you *ever* plan to tell me the truth?" Sabrina demanded.

"I—I didn't know the truth for sure."

"Of course you did. Why else were you so upset about the DNA testing?"

"I knew there was a possibility that Ben wasn't your father, but I never knew for sure. I never wanted to know." A tear rolled down her cheek.

"Well, now you do."

Her mother swallowed and brushed at her tears. Her hands were trembling.

Sabrina wanted to feel sorry for her mother, but she was too angry. She felt cheated. She had adored her father and even after learning about Glynnis and his other children, that adoration had remained. Now she felt completely abandoned. Her father was no longer her father, and her mother had betrayed her. "I have a right to know who my father is."

Her mother's expression was agonized. "Sabrina, I can't—"

"I'm not leaving until you tell me."

Isabel bit her bottom lip.

"I mean it."

Sighing deeply, her mother nodded. "Your father is Leland Fox."

Frozen, Sabrina whispered, "Oh, my God. Did… did Dad know?"

Her mother couldn't meet her eyes. "He may have guessed."

"And Leland? Does he know?"

"Yes."

"For how long?"

"He's always known it was possible. I'm so sorry, Sabrina. We never meant for you to find out."

Sabrina bowed her head.

"I want you to understand," her mother said in a stronger voice. "I've loved Leland from the time I was a girl. He was my beau all through school and my escort during my debutante season and although we went to different colleges, we had an understanding. Then, in our senior year, something happened. It was all my fault. We had a terrible fight and I gave him back his pin. I told him I didn't want to see him again.

"To pay me back, he started dating Cecily. I was hurt, so I began to date other boys, too. Before I knew what had happened, Leland and Cecily were married. I couldn't believe it. I met Ben right after that, and I married him on the rebound.

"When Leland finished law school, he and Cecily moved back to Rockwell, and gradually, we resumed our friendship. Before long, we…we became lovers again. When I got pregnant with you, I was terrified. I didn't know who had fathered you, but I wanted a child so badly, as did Ben, that I pushed my fears away and told myself it didn't matter who your biological father was. I was married to Ben, and legally, he would be your father.''

"You never considered how unfair that was to him? You didn't love him.''

"What else could I do? It wasn't as if I could divorce him and marry Leland. Leland and Cecily had just become parents for the second time, and if he had divorced Cecily and married me, the truth would all come out. Cecily would have made our lives hell. His kids would've ended up hating him. And the scandal in a town like this…'' Her eyes pleaded with Sabrina to understand. "I just couldn't face all that.''

"You thought it was better to live a lie.''

"It wasn't like that.''

"Yes, it was. And Dad knew it was all a lie. I heard him tell you that right before your accident.''

Sabrina felt sick to her stomach. Her mother hadn't stayed with Ben because she didn't believe in divorce or because she loved him or even because she wanted Sabrina to have a good life. She'd stayed with him because she didn't have a better option.

Bitterly, Sabrina wondered if she'd ever really known her mother at all. "You know, Mom,'' she said dully, "I gave up the only man I've ever loved because I didn't want to hurt you. Because I felt you'd been hurt enough, and because, as your daughter, I felt I owed you my loyalty. But everything I always believed in has been a lie. Everything.''

Sabrina closed her heart to her mother's cries as she rushed from the room and out of the house.

"Sabrina! What a pleasant surprise." Leland stood up as Sabrina entered his office. "Have a seat, my dear. What brings you here this morning?"

Sabrina waited until Leland's secretary had closed the door behind her before speaking. "My mother hasn't called you?"

Leland frowned. "Yes, she did, but I just got in from an appointment. I was about to call her. What's happened?"

"We got the results back from the DNA tests." Once again Sabrina repeated the information she'd been given by Dr. Zeller. She waited a heartbeat, then added, "My mother told me the truth."

Leland's shoulders slumped. "Everything?"

"Everything."

"I've always wanted you to know," he said softly. "I've always wanted to claim you as mine."

Whatever it was Sabrina had expected him to say, it wasn't this. But at the words, the hard knot in her chest began to melt. She swallowed, afraid to speak, afraid she'd break down and make a complete fool of herself.

Leland got up and came around to where she sat. He took her hands in his. "I know this has been a shock." Pulling her up, he put his arms around her.

His voice was gruff as he stroked her hair. "I want you to know the reason I stayed silent all these years wasn't because I cared about what other people thought.''

''My mother does.'' She couldn't keep the bitterness out of her voice.

He leaned back so he could see her face. ''Don't be too hard on her, Sabrina. She's not as strong as you are.''

Sabrina looked away. ''Why does everyone always make excuses for her?''

It took a moment for him to answer. ''Because we love her.''

Sabrina bit back a sob.

He gathered her close again and kissed her hair. ''I'm sorry you've been hurt. That's the last thing I ever wanted.'' Putting his hands on either side of her face, he looked into her eyes. ''I love you, sweetheart.''

Sabrina could no longer hold back the tears. So many conflicting emotions swirled inside her. All she wanted right then was to have this all be a dream. To wake up and be the person she'd always believed herself to be.

But that wasn't going to happen.

Her life had changed irrevocably this morning.

Now it was time to find out who this new Sabrina was and where she was going.

Chapter Thirteen

Gregg had been in a state of shock ever since Glynnis called him with the news about the DNA tests. At first he'd thought she was kidding.

Sabrina wasn't Ben's daughter.

It was hard to believe. They'd been very close. She'd thought the world of him, and even though she'd felt betrayed and hurt by the secrets he'd kept, Gregg knew she'd still loved him.

She must be devastated.

First Ben had let her down.

Now her mother had let her down.

You let her down, too.

Twice he picked up the phone to call her, and twice he put it down again. What could he say? That he was sorry about everything? Sorry he wasn't there for her when she needed him? Sorry he hadn't been more patient and understanding?

Gregg wondered what kind of showdown there'd been between Sabrina and her mother. And if Ben wasn't Sabrina's father, who was? Had Ben known?

These questions and others continued to gnaw at him as he tried to decide whether to call Sabrina or not. Finally the decision was made for him. Glynnis called to say she had received a call from Diane Clemmons. Diane informed her that Leland Fox wanted to meet with them the following day at his office.

"Will you go with me?" she asked.

"Of course."

"Sabrina will be there."

"I know. It's okay."

So he would see Sabrina the next day.

Would she forgive him?

And if she did, would she finally be willing to tell her mother the truth?

Sabrina debated and finally decided to go and see her mother in the morning before the meeting with Glynnis and the lawyers. Isabel wouldn't be there. Sabrina and Leland were representing her.

Sabrina didn't blame her mother for not wanting to attend. Why should she? She had no desire to be in Glynnis's company, plus Sabrina was sure she was deeply embarrassed and ashamed of the revelations the DNA testing had brought to light.

Some of Sabrina's anger and feelings of betrayal toward her mother had lessened over the past twenty-four hours. The bottom line was, she still loved her mother, and even though she couldn't condone her behavior, she did know what it was like to desperately love someone.

Gregg.

It hurt so much to think about him.

She didn't think he wanted anything more to do with her. She hadn't been brave enough to fight for their love, so in many ways she was just as cowardly as her mother had been, and she deserved to have lost him.

She accepted that.

Still, she had decided she wanted to make a clean breast of everything with her mother. If they were to have a good future relationship, it had to be built on honesty and trust. No more hiding. No more lying.

She called the house to tell her mother she was joining her for breakfast. ''Tell Florence I'm hoping she'll make me one of her Spanish omelettes.''

Sabrina felt a pang of pity when she arrived at the house. For the first time since she could remember, her mother wasn't impeccably turned out. It was obvious to Sabrina that Isabel had had a bad night. There were circles under her eyes, and she seemed tentative and subdued, not like herself at all.

She's suffering. She knows she was wrong, and

now she's afraid. Sabrina swallowed against the lump in her throat as she bent to embrace her mother. She could feel Isabel's body trembling as they hugged. And when the embrace was over, Sabrina saw tears shining in her mother's eyes.

"Let's go have our breakfast, then we'll talk, okay?" Sabrina said.

"All right."

By the time they reached the kitchen, Isabel was more composed. Elaine was already eating a bowl of cereal, and Florence was at the stove with all the omelette fixings ready to go. "Good morning," they both said.

"Good morning." Sabrina eyed Elaine's cereal. "You're not having one of Florence's omelettes?"

"I wish I could," the nurse said. "But even on medication, my cholesterol is too high. I've really got to watch it."

"She had a double bypass two years ago," Florence said.

"Really?" Sabrina was surprised. Elaine looked very fit and healthy.

"Yeah," Elaine said. "Don't ever smoke. That's what did it."

Sabrina smiled. "Don't worry. I can't stand the smell."

"I used to smoke," Isabel said.

Sabrina looked at her mother. "You did? I didn't know that."

"When I was in college. It was the cool thing to do then. Although we didn't say cool in those days."

Sabrina wondered how many other things about her mother she had never known.

They ate a leisurely breakfast, and when it was over, Sabrina and her mother retired to the sunroom. Sabrina closed the door behind them so they'd have complete privacy. They settled in, Isabel in a patch of sunlight by the window and Sabrina across from her in one of the comfortable armchairs dotted around the room.

"Sabrina," her mother began, "I thought about you all night. I hope you know how sorry I am about everything. I realize how much I've hurt you."

"It's all right, Mom. I'm okay."

"I know you went to see Leland after you left here yesterday."

"Yes."

"He was so pleased that you didn't seem to hate him. He loves you, you know. He told me once that he would be proud to claim you."

Sabrina was touched. "I like him, too. And maybe someday I'll feel more for him, but right now, it's too new."

"I know that." Isabel looked out the window. Once more a bird was feeding at the feeders, this time a black and white woodpecker with a red crown. "Sabrina, Leland has asked me to marry him when his divorce is final."

Sabrina nodded. She wasn't surprised. She had

half expected this even before she'd known her true parentage. "Are you going to?"

Now her mother met her gaze. "How would you feel about it if I did?"

"If marrying Leland will make you happy, I'm happy for you. Life is short, Mom. We have to make the most of it." But even as she said the words, Sabrina ached inside. Would she ever have a chance at happiness again?

Her mother's smile was tremulous…and grateful. "You're such a generous person. I'm…I'm lucky to have you as my daughter."

"I hope you feel that way after I tell you what I came here to tell you this morning."

Her mother's eyes widened.

"Like you, I had a sleepless night. I thought and thought about everything, and I made some decisions. The first is, I intend to sign over all my shares of the company stock to Dad's children."

"No! Sabrina, no! Your father…Ben…wouldn't have wanted you to do that. He loved you. He wanted you to have that stock."

"I've made up my mind, Mother."

"But Sabrina—"

"The second thing I wanted to tell you is that I am going to be giving my notice at the paper."

Her mother stared at her.

"I should have told you this a long time ago. Dad urged me to, but I was too much of a coward. I'm just not happy at the paper. I want to try other things.''

''What other things?''

''I want to write. I'm a journalist, not a CEO. I hate the business part of the paper.''

''If you want to write, then write. But that doesn't mean you have to quit.''

''Yes, it does. I can't do the kind of writing I want to do at the paper.''

''You…you won't leave Rockwell, will you?''

''I don't know. It all depends on a number of things.'' Sabrina took a long, deep breath. ''That brings me to the last and most important thing I have to tell you. About the man I was seeing. The one I told you about.''

''But—''

''Please just listen, okay? Don't say anything else until I finish telling you what I need to tell you. The man I was seeing, the man I fell in love with, is Gregg Antonelli. Glynnis Antonelli's brother.''

''Oh, my God.''

''After Dad died and Leland gave me his letter, I went to see Gregg. That's what Dad asked me to do, to go and see him and tell him what had happened so that Glynnis could get the news from Gregg and not some other way.''

Isabel's face had frozen. Sabrina knew she was shocked.

''Anyway, I met Gregg at the restaurant that he owns and I told him about Dad's death.'' Sabrina couldn't bring herself to say Ben instead of Dad. He had been her father in every way, and would always be her dad. "A couple of days later, Gregg called me and told me Glynnis wanted to meet me and she wanted me to meet the children. I wanted to go. I was curious about her and about the children. And, I have to admit, I wanted to see Gregg again, because from the moment we met, there was a strong attraction between us. I knew you would be very upset if you knew, so I didn't tell you."

Still her mother said nothing, and Sabrina saw the pain in her eyes.

Plunging on, she said, "I'm not saying this to hurt you, but if we're to go forward with any kind of hope for a good relationship, we have to be honest with each other from now on. That's the reason we're in such a mess now, because no one has been honest in our family. Not you, not Dad, not me. I don't want that anymore. Do you?"

"I—I'm sorry, I'm just so stunned."

"I know. Anyway, when I met Glynnis, I liked her a lot, and I loved the children. They're so sweet, and I thought of them…I *still* think of them…as my little brother and sister. But I didn't think I could see them again, because I didn't want to keep lying to you, and I could see no way around that. I knew you'd go crazy if you found out I was going to Ivy and spending time with them."

Her mother looked away. By the set of her chin, Sabrina knew how upset Isabel was.

"That day, when Gregg and I were saying good-bye, he blurted out that he wanted to see me again. He told me from the moment we'd met he'd known I was the woman he'd waited for all his life."

Isabel swallowed, but she didn't turn to look at Sabrina.

"Do you have any idea how seductive that was?" Sabrina said. "Especially since I was half in love with him already." She sighed heavily. "I know it was wrong to go behind your back, but I couldn't *not* see him. He began coming to Rockwell whenever he could get away, and several times, I went to Ivy. We became lovers very quickly. He asked me to marry him, but I couldn't see any way that that could ever be possible. I just couldn't bring myself to tell you about him. I figured you'd been hurt so much already, that Dad had betrayed you so badly, and I didn't want to betray you, too."

Finally her mother turned to look at her. "So you said no?"

"I never said no. I just couldn't see any way it would ever happen."

"That's what you meant yesterday when you said you'd given up the only man you ever loved because of me."

"Yes. He finally lost patience and gave me a kind of ultimatum, saying if I loved him enough, I'd tell you, and if I didn't, well, maybe it was better to know it then. So I promised I'd tell you that weekend. The weekend you fell and broke your arm."

Her mother grimaced.

"That just took all the wind out of my sails. I couldn't say anything after that. You were so miserable. I couldn't add to your pain. Gregg was very understanding. Very nice and very calm. But he said he thought it would be best if we didn't see each other anymore because it was too hard. That if I ever felt I could be honest with you about him, to call him. He didn't say he hoped it wasn't too late, but I knew that's what he was thinking."

"And have you seen him since?"

"Only in the courtroom."

"Have you spoken with him?"

"A few times. Very unsatisfactory conversations."

"So it's over, then."

"I don't know. I'm going to see him this afternoon, I'm sure. I don't think Glynnis will come to the meeting at Leland's office without him. I hope he still wants me, and if he does, I'm going to marry him. That's what I wanted to tell you. I hope you can accept that, because I want you to be a part of my life. If you can't, I'll be sad, but it won't change my mind." She felt so much better for having gotten all this out in the open. "I could have waited to see what Gregg said before telling you any of this, because if he doesn't want me, you wouldn't have had to know. But I'm tired of hiding things, especially something so important, something so integral to who I am."

For a long time, her mother was silent. Then she took a deep breath. "I hope, for your sake, he hasn't changed his mind. But Sabrina…" Now her eyes met Sabrina's. "I don't believe I am capable of being a part of your life if that life is spent with him."

Sabrina nodded slowly.

"I love you," her mother continued, "and I do want you to be happy, but I can't accept those people. I can't be one big happy family with them. It would never work."

Perhaps not, Sabrina thought. She wasn't sure what she felt. Regret and disappointment, but also acceptance. She hadn't really expected her mother to change overnight. Isabel was who she was, just as Sabrina was who she was. If the price of being with Gregg and having his children was a permanent estrangement from her mother, so be it. At least her mother didn't hate her. At least she'd wished her well. That was something.

Soon after, Sabrina left. She kissed her mother, told her she loved her and always would, no matter what happened.

"And I will always love you, no matter what happens."

Both had tears in their eyes as they said goodbye.

Sabrina was utterly calm when she entered Leland's office at one o'clock that afternoon. Finally telling her mother the truth about Gregg had been a turning point. She loved him desperately and hoped it wasn't too late for them, but if it was, she would accept his decision and move on.

As she'd said to her mother, life was short. Somehow she would try to build a satisfying life without him.

Still, her heart leaped at the sight of him. He and Glynnis were already seated, and both smiled warmly when she entered. The smiles made Sabrina feel better. At least neither was angry with her. Glynnis, as always, looked lovely, in a dark green wool pants outfit. And Gregg…well, he always looked wonderful. Today he wore casual khaki pants paired with a dark brown turtleneck sweater. Sabrina was glad she'd taken care with her appearance when she saw the approving look he gave her.

Their lawyer gave her only the briefest of nods, then said, "Now that everyone's here, shall we get started? I understand Mrs. March has dropped the suit."

"Yes," Leland said. He smiled at Sabrina. "Would you like some coffee, my dear?"

"No, thank you, Leland."

"I could ask Betty to bring you hot chocolate."

She gave him an affectionate smile. She might never get used to the fact he was her father, but she did like him very much. "No, it's okay. I just had lunch."

The Clemmons woman looked irritated. She looked at her watch, a beautiful Rolex. "I have another appointment at two, Leland."

"All right. I asked you all to come here because Sabrina has something she wants to tell you. Sabrina?"

Sabrina took a deep breath. She looked at Glynnis. "I've asked Leland to take care of something for me, and I wanted to tell you about it. I'm signing over all my shares in my father's…in Ben's company…to Michael and Olivia." At Glynnis's gasp and Gregg's startled look, she added, "I have no right to them. Ben wasn't my father, but he *is* theirs. The stock should belong to them."

Gregg and Glynnis exchanged a look. Then Gregg said, "Mr. Fox, is there somewhere Sabrina and I can be alone for a few minutes? There's something I have to discuss with her privately."

"Certainly." Leland reached over and pressed a button.

A moment later, Betty opened the door. "Yes, Mr. Fox?"

"Would you show Mr. Antonelli and Miss March into the library, please?"

"Of course." She smiled at Sabrina and Gregg. "Follow me."

Sabrina was afraid to hope, so she tried to keep her mind blank. Betty ushered them into the library, smiled and said, "If there's anything you want, just let me know."

"We're fine," Gregg said.

When the door closed behind Betty, he said, "Glynnis doesn't want your shares, Sabrina. She didn't even want the ones Ben left to the kids, but I wouldn't allow her to refuse them. All she wants is to go home and put all this behind her. That's all either of us want.''

Sabrina could hardly bear to look at him. It hurt too much. The faint hope she'd harbored since she'd made up her mind to tell her mother about them disappeared. In its place was a longing so strong, it was a physical pain. She had never felt this lonely in her life. Gregg and Glynnis would be going home to Ivy later today, and that would be that. She would never see either of them again.

The whole time these thoughts were running through her mind, Gregg watched her. And just as she realized this was the end, that he would never again hold her, never again kiss her, never again tell her he loved her, he reached out and pulled her into his arms.

Lifting her chin, he said, ''Sabrina, do you still love me?''

The question caused her heart to thump painfully. Looking into his eyes, she searched their depths. What she saw hollowed out her stomach. ''I'll always love you,'' she whispered.

''Can we get past this?''

''If you can, I can.''

His smile always had been her undoing. ''I can do anything if it means we can be together.''

As he captured her mouth in a kiss that lighted the dark places in her heart, Sabrina knew nothing else in the world mattered. Not what her father had done. Not what her mother did. Nothing.

All that mattered was Gregg and the love they felt for each other and the future they would build together.

A year later…

''Do you think she'll come?''

Sabrina looked at her husband, who was stocking the refrigerator with casseroles of lasagna from the restaurant in preparation for their daughter Samantha's christening party. ''I don't know. I hope so.''

They were discussing Sabrina's mother, who had still not acknowledged Gregg as her son-in-law. To spare Isabel and avoid the pain of a wedding her mother didn't attend, Sabrina had quickly wrapped up her affairs in Rockwell, then she and Gregg had flown to Hawaii where they'd been married quietly and spent a wonderful weeklong honeymoon relaxing in the sun. When they returned, they had a small reception in Ivy at Gregg's restaurant. Isabel sent a generous gift, but she did not attend.

Since then Sabrina had dutifully written and called her mother. But she hadn't gone to Rockwell to see her. Her mother had asked. She'd asked many times. But Sabrina had gone as far as she could go. The next step was up to her mother. And Sabrina had told her so.

Other than the estrangement from her mother, Sabrina was sublimely happy. In fact, she hadn't known a woman could be so happy. As she'd told Casey not two days ago, what more could any woman want?

Each day she counted her blessings, ticking them off in her head. A gorgeous, kind, loving husband. A beautiful baby daughter. A career she loved as a freelance journalist. A lovely home in Ivy, which was a beautiful city. A sister-in-law and niece and nephew that she loved dearly. Good friends. A full life. A wonderful life.

She smiled.

And had she mentioned the sex?

"What are you smiling about?" Gregg said.

"Sex," she said.

"Sex? Sex with who?"

"Whom."

"Sex with *whom*, you wanton thing." Walking over to her, he put his arms around her and caressed her bottom, giving her a suggestive grin.

"Sex with my sexy husband, of course." She grinned.

"It's a darn good thing you said that." He nuzzled her neck. "Um, you taste good. Samantha will probably sleep another hour. We've got time for a quickie."

"We do not. I have a million things to do before the party starts. Now stop that!" His hands had strayed to her breasts.

Sabrina, laughing, twisted away from him, even though she'd have liked nothing better than to go upstairs and climb into their big bed. "Tonight," she said.

"You promise?"

"I promise."

"I'll hold you to it."

"I'm counting on it."

"At least give me one kiss to tide me over."

"I know you. One kiss usually leads to two and before you know it, you've got me where you want me."

He gave her one of his sexy grins, and Sabrina almost said, *Oh, forget the party, let's go upstairs.* But better sense ruled.

For the next hour, they worked to finish getting ready, then Sabrina headed for the shower. By that time, Samantha was awake and Gregg said he'd tend to her until Sabrina was out of the shower and dressed.

At three o'clock, everything was done that needed doing, and they were ready for their guests. Samantha looked adorable in her christening dress. Her tuft of dark hair was pulled up into a "top tail" as Gregg called it and tied with a white satin ribbon.

Every time Sabrina looked at her, she was filled with an overwhelming love. Her blue-eyed darling, who looked so much like her father, was the light of her life.

Oh, if only Isabel could see her.

But it was her mother's choice not to. Sabrina constantly reminded herself of that fact. She'd done everything she could do. She'd called her mother the day after Samantha was born, and every time they'd talked since Sabrina had invited Isabel to come to Ivy. Six weeks had gone by, and her mother had still not come.

Sabrina determinedly pushed thoughts of her mother out of her mind. Today was not a day for sadness. Today was a day of joy.

Glynnis and the children were the first to arrive. Michael was six now and in the first grade. He was still just as sweet and serious as he'd always been. Olivia was four months shy of her third birthday and a handful, but everyone who knew her adored her. Livvy loved her baby cousin Samantha and couldn't wait until she was old enough to play with. Sabrina hugged and kissed all three. Aside from Gregg and Samantha, they were the most important people in her life, and she gave thanks for them every day.

After Glynnis came two of Sabrina and Gregg's friends with their children, followed by Gregg's cousin Steve and his new bride, Maggie, who worked for Gregg as his sous-chef.

Soon the house was filled with adults and children, all laughing and talking. Before Sabrina knew it, it was five o'clock and time to serve the food.

She had just taken the lasagna out of the oven when the doorbell rang.

Gregg and Sabrina looked at each other.

"I'll go," he said.

"No, I'll go. You start slicing the lasagna." Sabrina walked to the door and, after only a moment's hesitation, opened it.

Standing on the doorstep was a beaming Leland and beside him, sitting in her chair, was Sabrina's mother. Her smile was hesitant. ''Hi.''

''Oh, Mom.'' Sabrina's eyes filled. ''You came.''

''Am I still welcome?''

''You'll always be welcome.''

The next few minutes would forever remain a blur in Sabrina's mind. Leland and her mother coming inside. Meeting everyone. Saying hello to Gregg and then getting their first look at Samantha.

But when Gregg gently placed Samantha on Isabel's arms and she held her granddaughter for the first time, Sabrina knew she would never forget the look on her mother's face.

Gregg walked over to Sabrina and put his arm around her. At that moment, her heart was so full she was afraid it might burst.

''Thank you, God,'' she whispered. Then she raised her face for her husband's kiss.

* * * * *

If you enjoyed what you just read,
then we've got an offer you can't resist!

Take 2 bestselling love stories FREE!

Plus get a FREE surprise gift!

Clip this page and mail it to Silhouette Reader Service™

IN U.S.A.	IN CANADA
3010 Walden Ave.	P.O. Box 609
P.O. Box 1867	Fort Erie, Ontario
Buffalo, N.Y. 14240-1867	L2A 5X3

YES! Please send me 2 free Silhouette Special Edition® novels and my free surprise gift. After receiving them, if I don't wish to receive anymore, I can return the shipping statement marked cancel. If I don't cancel, I will receive 6 brand-new novels every month, before they're available in stores! In the U.S.A., bill me at the bargain price of $3.99 plus 25¢ shipping and handling per book and applicable sales tax, if any*. In Canada, bill me at the bargain price of $4.74 plus 25¢ shipping and handling per book and applicable taxes**. That's the complete price and a savings of at least 10% off the cover prices—what a great deal! I understand that accepting the 2 free books and gift places me under no obligation ever to buy any books. I can always return a shipment and cancel at any time. Even if I never buy another book from Silhouette, the 2 free books and gift are mine to keep forever.

235 SDN DNUP
335 SDN DNUS

Name	(PLEASE PRINT)	
Address	Apt.#	
City	State/Prov.	Zip/Postal Code

* Terms and prices subject to change without notice. Sales tax applicable in N.Y.
** Canadian residents will be charged applicable provincial taxes and GST.
  All orders subject to approval. Offer limited to one per household and not valid to
  current Silhouette Special Edition® subscribers.
  ® are registered trademarks of Harlequin Books S.A., used under license.

SPED02   ©1998 Harlequin Enterprises Limited

Your opinion is important to us! Please take a few moments to share your thoughts with us about your experiences with Harlequin and Silhouette books. Your comments will be very useful in ensuring that we deliver books you love to read. *Please take a few minutes to complete the questionnaire, then send it to us at the address below.*

Send your completed questionnaires to:
Harlequin/Silhouette Reader Survey, P.O. Box 9046, Buffalo, NY 14269-9046

1. As you may know, there are many different lines under the Harlequin and Silhouette brands. Each of the lines is listed below. Please check the box that most represents your reading habit for each line.

Line	Currently read this line	Do not read this line	Not sure if I read this line
Harlequin American Romance	❏	❏	❏
Harlequin Duets	❏	❏	❏
Harlequin Romance	❏	❏	❏
Harlequin Historicals	❏	❏	❏
Harlequin Superromance	❏	❏	❏
Harlequin Intrigue	❏	❏	❏
Harlequin Presents	❏	❏	❏
Harlequin Temptation	❏	❏	❏
Harlequin Blaze	❏	❏	❏
Silhouette Special Edition	❏	❏	❏
Silhouette Romance	❏	❏	❏
Silhouette Intimate Moments	❏	❏	❏
Silhouette Desire	❏	❏	❏

2. Which of the following best describes why you bought *this book?* One answer only, please.

the picture on the cover	❏	the title	❏
the author	❏	the line is one I read often	❏
part of a miniseries	❏	saw an ad in another book	❏
saw an ad in a magazine/newsletter	❏	a friend told me about it	❏
I borrowed/was given this book	❏	other: _____	❏

Where did you buy *this book?* One answer only, please.

at Barnes & Noble	❏	at a grocery store	❏
at Waldenbooks	❏	at a drugstore	❏
at Borders	❏	on eHarlequin.com Web site	❏
at another bookstore	❏	from another Web site	❏
at Wal-Mart	❏	Harlequin/Silhouette Reader	❏
at Target	❏	Service/through the mail	
at Kmart	❏	used books from anywhere	❏
at another department store or mass merchandiser	❏	I borrowed/was given this book	❏

On average, how many Harlequin and Silhouette books do you buy at one time?

I buy _____ books at one time	❏
I rarely buy a book	❏

MRQ403SSE-1A

5. How many times per month do you shop for any *Harlequin and/or Silhouette* books?
One answer only, please.

1 or more times a week	❑	a few times per year	❑
1 to 3 times per month	❑	less often than once a year	❑
1 to 2 times every 3 months	❑	never	❑

6. When you think of your ideal heroine, which *one* statement describes her the best?
One answer only, please.

She's a woman who is strong-willed	❑	She's a desirable woman	❑
She's a woman who is needed by others	❑	She's a powerful woman	❑
She's a woman who is taken care of	❑	She's a passionate woman	❑
She's an adventurous woman	❑	She's a sensitive woman	❑

7. The following statements describe types or genres of books that you may be
interested in reading. Pick *up to 2 types* of books that you are most interested in.

I like to read about truly romantic relationships
I like to read stories that are sexy romances
I like to read romantic comedies
I like to read a romantic mystery/suspense
I like to read about romantic adventures
I like to read romance stories that involve family
I like to read about a romance in times or places that I have never seen
Other: _____

*The following questions help us to group your answers with those readers who are
similar to you. Your answers will remain confidential.*

8. Please record your year of birth below.
19 _____

9. What is your marital status?
single ❑   married ❑   common-law ❑   widowed
divorced/separated ❑

10. Do you have children 18 years of age or younger currently living at home?
yes ❑   no ❑

11. Which of the following best describes your employment status?
employed full-time or part-time ❑   homemaker ❑   student
retired ❑   unemployed ❑

12. Do you have access to the Internet from either home or work?
yes ❑   no ❑

13. Have you ever visited eHarlequin.com?
yes ❑   no ❑

14. What state do you live in?
_____

15. Are you a member of Harlequin/Silhouette Reader Service?
yes ❑   Account # _____   no ❑   MRQ403SSE

SPECIAL EDITION™

MONTANA MAVERICKS

The Kingsleys

Nothing is as it seems
beneath the big skies of Montana.

HER MONTANA MILLIONAIRE
by Crystal Green
(Silhouette Special Edition #1574)

New York socialite Jinni Fairchild was barely surviving Rumor's slow pace. Until she met Max Cantrell. Tall. Dark. Gorgeous. And rich as Midas. Would his unhurried sensuality tempt this fast-lane girl to stop and smell the roses—with him?

Available November 2003 at your favorite retail outlet.

COMING NEXT MONTH

SSECNM1